The Girl on the Ferryboat

ANGUS PETER CAMPBELL

Luath Press Limited

EDINBURGH

www.luath.co.uk

First published 2013
New edition 2014
Reprinted 2019

ISBN: 978-1-910021-18-7

The publisher acknowledges the support of

ALBA | CHRUTHACHAIL

towards the publication of this book.

The author's right to be identified as author of this book
under the Copyright, Designs and Patents Act 1988 has been asserted.

The paper used in this book is recyclable. It is made from
low chlorine pulps produced in a low energy, low emissions manner
from renewable forests.

Printed and bound by
Bell & Bain Ltd., Glasgow

Typeset in 10.5 point Sabon

The Greatest Gift, Fountain Publishing,1992
Cairteal gu Meadhan-Latha, Acair Publishing, 1992
One Road, Fountain Publishing, 1994
Gealach an Abachaidh, Acair Publishing, 1998
Motair-baidhsagal agus Sgàthan, Acair Publishing, 2000
Lagan A' Bhàigh, Acair Publishing, 2002
An Siopsaidh agus an t-Aingeal, Acair Publishing, 2002
An Oidhche Mus Do Sheòl Sinn, Clàr Publishing, 2003
Là a' Dèanamh Sgèil Do Là, Clàr Publishing, 2004
Invisible Islands, Otago Publishing, 2006
An Taigh-Samhraidh, Clàr Publishing, 2007
Meas air Chrannaibh/ Fruit on Branches, Acair Publishing, 2007
Tilleadh Dhachaigh, Clàr Publishing, 2009
Suas gu Deas, Islands Book Trust, 2009
Archie and the North Wind, Luath Press, 2010
Aibisidh, Polygon, 2011
An t-Eilean: Taking a Line for a Walk, Islands Book Trust, 2012
Fuaran Ceann an t-Saoghail, Clàr Publishing, 2012
An Nighean air an Aiseag, Luath Press, 2013
Memory and Straw, Luath Press, 2017
Stèisean, Luath Press, 2018
Constabal Murdo, Luath Press, 2018

ANGUS PETER CAMPBELL is from South Uist. After local school at Garrynamonie Primary and Daliburgh Junior Secondary he went to Oban High School where his English teacher was Iain Crichton Smith. From there he went to Edinburgh University where he graduated with Double Honours in Politics and History. He has worked as a newspaper, radio and television journalist and his literature has gained several awards. His Gaelic novel *An Oidhche Mus Do Sheòl Sinn* was shortlisted for the Scottish Book of the Year Award in 2004 and publicly voted into the top 10 of the best-ever books from Scotland in the Orange/List Awards of 2007. His poetry collection *Aibisidh* was the Scottish Poetry Book of the Year in 2011 and *Memory and Straw* won the Saltire Society Scottish Fiction Book of the Year Award in 2017.

for Liondsaidh and the children with love
Salm CXV111 *mar thaing*

'Though there be no such thing as Chance in the world, our ignorance of the real cause of any event has the same influence on the understanding, and begets a like species of belief or opinion.'
David Hume, *An Enquiry Concerning Human Understanding*

Acknowledgements

Thanks to Kirsten Graham, Jennie Renton, Louise Hutcheson and Gavin MacDougall of Luath Press for their editorial advice and support. To the Gaelic Books Council who supported the Gaelic version of this novel, also published by Luath. My gratitude to all those, such as Norma Campbell of Kingussie and Inverness, Ryno Morrison of Lewis, Dr John MacInnes of Raasay and Edinburgh, Dolina MacLennan of Lewis and Edinburgh, and Angus MacLeod of Rudh' Aisinis, South Uist, who gave me little snippets which appear here. I am indebted, as always, to Fr Allan MacDonald's lovely book *Words and Expressions from South Uist and Eriskay* (Dublin: The Institute for Advanced Studies, 1958). My biggest thanks, as ever, to my wife Liondsaidh and our children for all their love, and for generously giving me the time and freedom to write this book.

I

IT WAS A LONG hot summer: one of those which stays in the memory forever. I can still hear the hum of the bees, and the call of the rock pigeons far away, and then I heard them coming down from the hill.

Though it wasn't quite like that either, for first I heard the squeaking and creaking in the distance, as if the dry earth itself was yawning before cracking. Don't you remember – how the thin fissures would appear in the old peat bogs towards the middle of spring?

A gate opened, and we heard the clip-clop of the horse on the stones which covered The Old Man's Ditch, just out of sight. An Irishman, O'Riagan, was the Old Man – some poor old tinker who'd once taken a dram too many and fell into the ditch, never to rise.

Then they appeared – Alasdair and Kate, sitting gaily on top of the peat bags in the cart. He wearing a small brown bunnet, with a clay pipe stuck in his mouth, while she sat knitting beside him, singing. The world could never be improved. Adam and Eve never ate that apple, after all.

They were building their first boat, though neither of them were young.

At the time, I myself was very young, though I didn't know it then. The university behind me and the world before me, though I had no notion what to do with it. I had forever, with the daylight pouring out on every side from dawn till dusk, every day without end, without beginning.

I saw her first on the ferry as we sailed up through the Sound of Mull. Dark curly hair and freckles and a smile as bonny as the machair. Her eyes were blue: we looked at each other as she climbed and I descended the stairs between the deck and the restaurant. 'Sorry,' I said to her, trying to stand to one side, and she smiled and said, 'O, don't worry – I'll get by.'

I wanted to touch her arm as she passed, but I stayed my hand and she left. My sense is that she disembarked at Tobermory, though it could have been at Tiree or Coll. For in those days the boat called at all these different places which have now melted into one. Did the boat tie up alongside the quay, or was that the time they used a small fender with the travellers ascending or descending on iron ropes?

Maybe that was another pier somewhere else, some other time.

Algeciras to Tangier: I think that was the best voyage I ever made, that time I caught a train down through Spain, the ferry across to Tangier, and another train from there through the red desert down to Casablanca. Everything shimmered in the haze: I recall music and an old man playing draughts at a disused station and the gold minarets of Granada shining as we passed through.

The windows were folded down as we travelled through Morocco, with men in long white kaftans bent over the fields. I ran out of money and a young Berber boy who was also travelling paid my fare before disappearing into the crowd. That was in my third year at university, a while before time existed.

I walked over to where Alasdair and Kate and the horse and cart had now come into sight. 'There you are, Eochaidh,' I said to the pony, stroking the mane.

'Aye aye,' the old man said as we walked over to the stream to water the horse.

While Eochaidh drank his world, Alasdair and Kate and I carried the peat bags to the stack. They would shape her later. Kate made the lunch and the four of us sat round the table eating ham and egg and slices of cheese and pickle.

Big Roderick they called my boss – the best boatmaker in the district when he was sober, who would occasionally go astray before returning to work with renewed vigour, as if the whole world needed to be created afresh. At this time we were at the beginning of creation: all revelation still lay ahead.

I was just a labourer. Big Roderick's servant.

'The tenon saw,' he'd shout now and again, and I'd run and get hold of that particular kind. The one with the thin rip-files for cutting across the grain. That was for the early, rough part of the work before the finesse set in and his ancient oak box with the polished chisels emerged to frame and bevel and pare and dovetail.

'How are you getting on?' Alasdair asked.

'O,' said Roderick, 'no reason to complain. You'll be launched by midsummer.'

'Blessings,' said Alasdair. 'Didn't I tell them there was no one like you this side of the Clyde?'

'Isn't truth lovely?' said Kate.

She was called Katell at the beginning. Katell Pelan from Becherel in Brittany, but who had now travelled the world with this little man she'd married nearly fifty years ago. Since they'd first met in a house in Edinburgh where she'd been a student but working in Bruntsfield as a servant girl and he cleaning the windows before starting his apprenticeship. A while then in Leith when he worked at Henry Robb's shipyards, and Clydebank after that under the shadow of John Brown's, before they went to Belfast and Harland & Wolff and the long years when he was at deep sea and the children came. First the bits of Breton and Gaelic then their mutual English and at last, here they were at the end of the journey, which had come so suddenly.

Big Roderick and I were caulking the carvel planks with oakum, fitted between the seams and the hull. How simple building a boat was: like a jigsaw. You only had to use common sense. Put one part next to another.

'Logic, boy,' Big Roderick would say, 'you just add bit to bit and before you know it you have a boat.'

Though we both knew fine that nothing was that simple. The difficulty of course was in knowing which bits fitted where, which bits made sense.

We rested a while by the unfinished stern, looking out west towards the Atlantic. A large vessel of some kind was sailing north.

'So,' he said then. 'And did you learn anything of worth at that university of yours?'

Well, what would I say? That I hadn't? – the great lie. Or that I had? – the bigger lie. Sartre and Marx and Hegel and all the rest.

'Yes,' I said, 'though I'm not very sure what use it'll do me.'

He lifted the gouge from his apron. 'Never tell me that a thing is of no use. You got a chance I never had. With this gouge I can shape wood. But with your education...'

He stood up, pointing to the vessel which was far out at sea.

'The day will come,' he said, 'when there will be no day like this. When we'll all be strangers and we won't believe a thing. Keep your education for that day.'

And we continued shaping the wood for the rest of the day.

2

THE GIRL ON the ferryboat was called Helen: she'd been visiting friends in Edinburgh and when she turned round, the violin was gone forever.

Waverley Station.

She'd only put it down on the bench for a moment as she searched for her purse, and when she looked back it had disappeared. She had that moment of disbelief: she must have left it at home, on the high shelf at the bottom of the bed above the bay window overlooking the garden, or perhaps out in the garden shed itself, where she now practised on warm summer days. Except it was now November.

No one in the world noticed, for it continued as before. It was 8.20am, the very middle of the rush hour. Everyone ran. No one carried a violin under their arm. A terrible piper busked over by Platform 17, where the train from Euston was due. An old man, still drunk from the night before, lay slumped on the bench. She wanted to shake him awake, but of course he wouldn't know.

She searched everywhere. Beneath and behind and beside the bench. Round every other bench and seat. All over the concourse and in every shop. In the bins and toilets. She told a station guard, who told her to tell the police. The officer on duty added the fiddle to the endless list. 'Go and try all the pawn shops,' he suggested, helpfully giving her all the addresses.

None of them had been given a fiddle, and though she went back to every pawn shop in the city every day for the next three months, the tune was always the same: Sorry, Miss.

She visited nearby cities, visiting and revisiting all the pawn shops there too, but no one had seen the instrument. She advertised in the newspapers and in shop windows, but no one responded.

It had been in the family for generations, brought back from Naples by her great-grandfather on her mother's side sometime in the 1880s. Though it was no Stradivarius, it made a beautiful sound: deep and mellow, yet bright and tuneful.

'An angel made it', the old people used to say and began to compare it to the famous chanter played by the MacKinnon family, which had been made by the fairies in Dunvegan. Nobody but a MacKinnon could play that chanter, and whenever anyone else touched it, it lost all its music.

It was given to young James MacKinnon on the way back from the Battle of Sheriffmuir. Wounded just above the left knee he still managed to hirple north, washing himself in the burns and feeding on oats and water. One night as he was crossing the Moor of Rannoch he heard a whimpering noise in the heather. A woman was dying with a child in her arms.

'Take this child home to Skye,' the woman said to him. And she also handed him a pouch. 'And if you ever find yourself in desperate straits just use this and all danger will flee. But don't open it until in real need.'

As he walked through Glencoe with the child in his arms, a terrible snowstorm fell. Collapsing in the drifts, he managed to untie the pouch to find the silver chanter. Raising it to his lips, he blew and instantly the snow ceased and a beautiful starlit night emerged. The young boy child turned out to be a MacCrimmon from the famous piping dynasty: their magic was also that of the MacKinnons.

Helen's great-grandfather was a sailor in the days when ships were made of oak and canvas. Rumour had it that he'd sold a crew member in exchange for the violin, but that was mere envy on the part of those who watched him become a famous musician on his return from voyaging overseas. He became a favourite of Queen Victoria's, and an iconic photograph of Her Majesty with Scott Skinner on one side and Archibald Campbell on the other can still be found in the vaults of the National Portrait Gallery in Edinburgh.

She herself was twelve when she was given the fiddle by her mother. After Archibald died it was played for a while by his youngest son, Fearchar, but when he died with the millions of others in the trenches, the fiddle fell silent for two generations. Helen's mother found it one day in the loft of the byre beneath a pile of old straw and had it restored, first of all by George Smith the local carpenter, and then by the London firm of violin repair specialists, Deroille and Sons of Charing Cross.

Their leading repairer, Vincent Deroille, was so impressed by the violin that he tried to buy it, but Helen's mother refused, telling him that it was a family heirloom which would never leave the family as long as she was alive. Which of course was something of a reimagined history, given that it had lain uncared for in the byre for nearly a century.

'Not to worry,' her mother said when she phoned to tell her the news.

'It's an impossible thing to lose. It may have gone out of our sight, but his eye will still be upon it.'

This omnipotent eye was her grandfather's, which still kept a close watch on the fiddle from beyond the grave.

'It will burn in the thief's hands,' she said. 'The instrument will refuse to play.'

This faith was not an unreasonable thing. Had not everything that had ever been stolen ultimately not turned into ashes? Was it just some kind of strange coincidence that her own sister's husband had died no sooner than he remarried? And what about that time the minister's motorcycle was stolen from outside the manse, only for them to find the bike and rider at the bottom of the ravine the following Sunday?

She was on her way home now to deal with it all. Not the loss of the instrument, of course, but the grief and the story which lay behind all of that. She decided to take the bicycle. Her hands felt safer that way, gripping something solid, pushing it gently along the platform at Queen Street. How beautifully the spokes turned as she wheeled it along. The red Raleigh badge flashed with each revolution.

She put the bike in the guard's van and sat by the window in carriage B, seat number 24. Not that any of that mattered: she just noticed it. Westerton and Dalmuir and Dumbarton Central, then the long familiar curve and climb through Helensburgh Upper, Garelochhead and Arrochar and Tarbert.

She read Pynchon and stared out the window. The hazels bent towards the windows. They were the best trees too for preventing landslides. Their long roots held in the thinnest of soils, binding the loosest things together.

Mull was where they'd finally settled, though settled might be too staid a word for it. A croft no less, or at least a smallholding, where her mother had gone 'back to the earth' and brought the four of them up self-sufficiently in a heaven of pigs and hens and goats and sheep and cattle and horses, in a paradise of oats and grain and carrots and leeks and potatoes and herbs.

How gorgeous it was to wake up in the morning to that smell of bread. How you took the cream off the milk and kept it in wooden basins in the shade until the whey separated from the curds and the marvel – the ingenuity! – of that home made churn which slowly transformed it all into butter. The dirtier the potatoes from out the ground the better. She smiled. How sweet the first tiny tomatoes always tasted, and as she closed her eyes she could see the apples and pears falling, one by one, into her sister's wicker basket. Mull, the lovely Officers' Mess.

Her ambition as a child was to be a watchmaker. She was fascinated by them: how the numbers always remained fixed while everything else moved. The hour hand invisibly, the minute hand ever so slowly, the second hand always fast and steady. She would close her eyes and count to sixty, but she could never get it exactly right. As she spoke sixty, the seconds hand would always either be moving towards fifty-nine or just one second past the top.

Her mother had a beautiful gold watch with Roman dials which Helen loved. She'd remove it and leave it behind on the dresser any time she went out to work in the fields and Helen would then always try it on. It was too big, but if she wound the leather strap twice round it fitted halfway up her arm perfectly. The numerals were diamond studded and luminous and Helen would crawl into the cupboard beneath the stairs where they would shine green in the darkness.

She remembered going into the old clockmaker's shop in Tobermory where time was completely fluid. Archie had dozens of clocks on the walls, all showing different times. A handwritten sign under each one taught you that while it was 12 noon in Tobermory it was 2pm in Berlin, 7pm in Kuala Lumpur, and 6am in New York.

Numerous clocks and watches lay open on the long wooden work bench that ran all the way beneath the windows. 'Would you like a look?' Archie asked her and she nodded, and he handed her the magnifying glass he used himself and she disappeared into a gigantic world of wheels and spokes and hooks and wires.

'See,' Archie said, 'if you do this – see what happens,' and he touched the edge of a wheel with a needle and it moved, catching the wheel next to it until it locked and the two wheels spun, dancing. 'Try it.' And she touched this and that moved, and touched that and the other thing and another thing and another thing moved.

'We'll make a watch,' her mother said to her on the way back home and they went down to the shore to gather shells. Tiny little corals of all shapes and sizes which the two of them then strung together once they got back home and tied together with a thin thread of lace. 'There,' her mother said to her. 'Now it can be any time for you.' And of course like all of us she made daisy watches and blew the seeds off a dandelion to find the right time: blow hard and it was early, soft and it would be late.

I must have travelled on the earlier train, otherwise I would have seen her then. She was very beautiful, with natural auburn hair and freckles, though that's only a haphazard brushstroke. She was studying Ecology, doing her thesis on the nature of the native woodlands of the south-west of Mull.

This was a familiar journey. Once off the train, the left turn down by the shellfish stall across the wooden pier, then the sail out past Kerrera with the Lynn of Lorne and Lismore to the starboard side, Kingairloch and Morvern ahead. Kingairloch from Ceann Geàrr Loch, the head of the half-loch.

As she sat sunglassed on deck I must have been below in the steerage, drinking. It was all whisky in those days, with accordion music and yelping dogs and returning sailors singing about South Georgia, though some of the drovers on their way to the South Uist cattle sales sang their own songs:

'O, gin I were far Gaudie rins, far Gaudie rins, far Gaudie rins, O gin I were far Gaudie rins at the back o Bennachie,' and up the Sound of Mull with a drunkard standing on one of the tables crying, 'Fareweel tae Tarwathie, adieu Mormond Hill, And the dear land o Crimmond I bid thee fareweel, I am bound now for Greenland and ready to sail, In the hopes I'll find riches a-hunting the whale...'

I needed air. Fresh air. Up on deck the heather on Mam Chullaich was still singed from the muirburning and the sky a clear blue to the north-west, where everything lay. I was hungry and made for the restaurant downstairs.

She was at the bottom of the steps as I descended. Dark curly hair and freckles and a smile that split the skies. We looked at each other as she climbed and I descended.

'Sorry,' I said to her, trying to stand to one side, and she smiled and said, 'O, don't worry – I'll get by.'

I wanted to touch her arm as she passed, but I stayed my hand and she left.

I think I just had soup, though I can't really remember. I may have gone to the bar afterwards, or reclimbed the stairs up to the deck area to look for her, but she wasn't there. The boat berthed first at Tobermory where hundreds of passengers, mostly tourists, disembarked. Others disembarked at Coll and Tiree and Castlebay and of course she must have come off with the crowd at one of these ports for I never saw her again.

I remember a girl carrying a bicycle over her shoulder at one of the ports, descending the ramp cautiously then jumping swiftly on to the bike at the bottom of the gangway and heading off across the pier, dodging round the porters.

Once she left the pier she ascended the hill past the hotel and out the old mill road past the brewery which took her to the single-track road to Dervaig and on to Calgary. It was a May morning and the ditches overflowed with buttercups and primroses. The sounds of birds filled the air: she knew them all by note. Thrushes and willow warblers and linnets and goldencrests. The finches high overhead. The plovers swooping up and down beside her through the glen. The smell of wild garlic filled her nostrils. O God, the glorious days before traffic.

Her mother was milking Daisy down by the gate. She still looked like a young girl herself, her long hair, though now flecked with grey, blowing in the breeze. Helen stopped at the top of the brae listening to the scene: the endless songs of the birds, the wind in the silver birches, the sound of the milk squirting into the pail. Her mother sensed her there and turned, still sitting on her stool, and waved. She cycled down towards her and stroked Daisy as the milk continued to flow.

Inside, they embraced.

'It's so lovely to see you, *a ghràidh*,' her mother said, smiling. 'You look wonderful.'

'You too,' said Helen. 'All that fresh air.'

They made tea and had some scones.

'How's Glasgow?'

'Oh – so so. As you would expect. All noise and fun. And pollution.'

'Studying hard? Not that it really matters.'

'Yes. No. Not because it matters but... because it matters.'

They both smiled.

'So,' her mother said, 'you lost the fiddle.'

'Yes. Sorry.'

'As I said on the phone, it doesn't matter. It'll turn up. Someplace. Sometime.'

'I'm sorry,' said Helen again. 'It was just a moment. Seconds really and that was it.'

'It always is.'

'Shall we go outside?' Helen asked. 'Into the orchard?'

She was talking about the death of her father. Helen was then only five. There was no reason for it really – just an ordinary day, no wind to speak of, but the line somehow got snagged on the winch and she went down in seconds according to the coastguards.

'When we lose something,' her mother was saying, 'it always goes somewhere. Nothing ever just dissolves. You know the Gaelic saying?' *"Thig trì nithean gun iarraidh...?"* 'Three things come unsought – fear, jealousy and love.'

'And which of these...?' asked Helen.

Her mother smiled.

'All three, of course. Though not necessarily in that order.' She stood up and plucked an apple from the tree. 'I loved him immensely. And I feared for him immensely. And I jealously guarded him from himself. Though I failed. For we always fail.'

She put the apple down with the others in the wooden press, and turned the handle to squeeze out the juice which trickled into the jar below.

They walked arm in arm out through the willow arch and began climbing the brae at the back of the house. The collie dog, Glen, joined them, always hopeful. They rested at the top of the hill looking westwards towards Coll where the boat on which I stood was sailing, at that moment passing Rudha Sgùrr Innis and the Eilean Mòr, making for the open sea.

3

WHEN HE WAS nine, Alasdair's grandfather took him out sea-fishing for the first time.

It was the first Saturday of the summer holidays, and all the more glorious because he had no notion it was going to happen. The sound of the heavy rain on the zinc roof woke him and when he looked outside through the tiny attic window the sky was dank and heavy.

He climbed back into his closet and lay on his back listening to the drumbeats of the rain. It rattled against the zinc, then if he listened really carefully he could hear it separating at the ridges and running in streams down the vents to the eaves. He raced them against each other. There were five vents to each corrugated sheet. He focused on the one above his head. The outside vent was Paavo Nurmi. In vent two was Jesse Owens. Joie Ray in vent three. Jackson Scholz in four and the Albannach, Eric Liddell, in the inside lane.

Off they went, Roy running so fast downhill but quickly overtaken by Scholz in lane four, and then came Owens and Liddell, each keeping pace with the other, step by step, but in the last sudden rush down to the eaves the great Paavo Nurmi won, once again, and the race started all over again.

When he woke the second time all was quiet and still. He heard his grandfather's voice downstairs so he immediately jumped out of bed, dressed in seconds, and was with him before his voice died away.

'Alasdair!' his grandfather said. 'We thought the fairies had taken you away during the night! What kept you so long?'

'The race,' he said. 'It was fantastic. Nurmi won again!'

His grandfather smiled.

'One day, Alasdair, you'll run as fast as him too. Now – where's your stuff?'

'Stuff?'

'Aye. Your stuff.'

'Oh,' said Alasdair, running out into the byre.

He climbed the wooden ladder up into the drying straw where the rod was hidden. His grandfather had made it for him last winter, just as the snow had settled in. They'd gone out rabbit hunting in the afternoon and instead of taking the usual shore road home had cut east through the only surviving wood in the area. 'Birch or hazel would be best,' his grandfather said, 'but we'll just make do with whatever has fallen.'

They searched for ages, but each fallen branch that Alasdair brought back was somehow deficient – too small, or too thick, or too soft, or too brittle – but finally he found a long thin willow twig which his grandfather said was 'perfect'.

'You carry it home,' his grandfather said, and no prouder soldier ever marched with his rifle held firmer over his shoulder. He was Alasdair MacColla and Gille-Pàdraig Dubh and Robin Hood and Daniel Boone all rolled into one.

Back home, his grandfather took out his whittling knife and helped him shear off the sprigs and nodules.

'Now let's soak it in the old feeding tub overnight.'

The old feeding tub was filled with sheep's urine ready for softening the tweed.

'It'll make the wood nice and pliable.'

And it did. By morning, Alasdair could bend and manipulate the willow rod any way he wanted.

'You want it that way to bear all the salmon you'll catch!' his grandfather said to him.

And then as the snow fell for days on end the two of them

sat by the fire slitting the rod, fitting the thread, turning the weaving thrums into fishing spindles, and seasoning and polishing the rod.

He now grabbed it out of the straw and jumped down from the byre ladder with it.

'It's only for show,' his grandfather said. 'We're not going to the river today. But don't tell your mother. We'll keep it as a surprise for her later. Let's eat first.'

He walked with his grandfather down by the peat stack and across the moor road which took them by the river and the twin lochs. But once out of sight of the house his grandfather turned east and led him down through the small ravine which separated the moorland from the grazing slopes. They clambered over the rocks until they reached the heights of the bay overlooking the sea. It glittered silver far below them. To the far south they could see the small hills of Barra blue on the horizon. Out west all was ocean as far as America. Beyond the bay itself, the mountains of Skye ascended into the air.

'Are we?' Alasdair thought, but didn't speak the words out loud. His grandfather – how nimbly he moved! – led the way downhill. Almost running, really. They reached the bay where his boat lay. *Reul-na-Mara* it was called – The Star of the Sea. The number of times Alasdair had dreamt of this moment: of standing here with his grampa beside the boat, ready to sail forth.

'Up you go,' he said, lifting Alasdair into the boat in one movement. 'You hold that rope,' he said, and the world began.

His grandfather took to the oars while Alasdair sat in the stern at the imagined tiller. His grandfather rowed steadily, taking the wee boat out of the harbour, round the skerry on which the seals basked. Alasdair could see the sandy bottom through the strands of seaweed. Millions of tiny fish, no bigger than his own pinky, moved beneath the water.

'They're called *siolagain*,' his grandfather said. 'Sand eels. Can you count them?'

Alasdair tried.

'A million,' he said. 'And one.'

Once they'd cleared the skerries his grandfather offered him the oars.

'Sit right there,' he said. 'Square-on in the middle. And hold this one like that – that's it – right between the thumb and the palm, and I'll row with the other one until you get used to it.'

Alasdair splashed and thrashed the water pointlessly, but eventually got the hang of slicing the oar in at the backward angle until it furrowed in through the water then rose again.

'Try this one as well,' his grandfather said, handing him the other oar. It took even longer to coordinate the oars as they went round in tiny circles. But his grampa seemed quite relaxed about it all, lighting his pipe and sitting in the stern. Eventually Alasdair managed to move the boat forwards with balanced little strokes which stirred the water around them.

'Keep your eye on that point over there,' his grandfather said, 'and row towards it. You can't go wrong.'

Alasdair kept his eye fixed on the landmark he had given him, the roof of the old church at Eolaigearraidh which stood on the highest hill in the distance. His arms and hands ached but he would never let his grandfather know. Paavo Nurmi never tired.

Suddenly they appeared on the near horizon, leaping high out of the ocean.

'Whales!' he cried. 'Grampa – look! Whales!'

A whole school of them lay ahead making rainbows in the sky.

'*Mucan-biorach, a' bhalaich,*' his grandfather said, smiling. 'Dolphins, lad. Though we have dozens of different names for them in our tongue – *leumadairean, deilfean, bèistean-ghorm, peallaichean...* depending on which kind they are.'

He cupped his old hands round his eyes.

'These look like *mucan-biorach* to me. Aren't they beautiful? *An giomach, an rionnach 's an ròn – trì seòid a' chuain!* The lobster, the mackerel and the seal – the three heroes of the ocean! Whoever spoke such nonsense! You'll never see a more beautiful sight on all the earth than these dolphins leaping before you.'

Alasdair wanted to hear his stories again, and grandfather knew it.

'*Innis dhomh mun deidhinn* – tell me about them. Please.' said Alasdair, and his grandfather once again began telling of how he'd sailed round Cape Horn in the sailing ship.

'I was fifteen days up there, in the crow's nest, icicles hanging from my beard.'

Alasdair knew that the icicles grew longer each time he told the story.

'How long were they?'

'Oh,' said his grampa, 'this long.' And he stretched his arms out as wide as he could. 'They were hanging from my chin down to below my knees,' he said. 'The ship's master had to saw them off with heated shears.'

Nearer, Alasdair could clearly see that the dolphins were not black at all, as they first appeared, but grey and blue. It was impossible to count how many there were, for each time two or three dived, another two or three surfaced. At any given time seven or eight of them leapt high into the air in semicircles.

'Wow!' he said to himself, under his breath. 'Wait till I tell this to Donald and Seumas.'

'It's also a good sign,' his grandfather said, 'that there's plenty of fish around.' He lifted the sacking which lay at his feet and there, hidden beneath, were the handlines.

'One for you, and one for the *bodach*,' his grandfather said, giving one of the handlines to Alasdair. It was an empty rectangle of wood encased in hooked twine.

'Careful as you release that twine,' he said, and the two of them sat side by side, unwinding the twine which had a hook attached every foot or so. Grandfather raised the other bit of sacking at his feet and revealed the enclosed box of bait.

'Plenty there to keep us going all day,' he said, and the two of them began to place the herring heads and livers and worms on the hooks. 'You never know,' his grandfather said, 'what they'll bite, so for this first cast we'll put different bait on different hooks.'

He taught Alasdair how to safely release the line into the water and let it drift.

'The sea itself will do the work for you. You'll feel the tugs,' he said, 'and when you do, just start hauling in.'

Alasdair watched as baited hook after baited hook disappeared behind them into the blue sea. For the first haul, grandfather allowed him to hold the wood.

'Just roll it clockwise,' he told Alasdair, and as he did so the line began to rise up. They took a few mackerel on that first cast, all on the worm. 'Ah!' his grampa said, '*Latha nam Boiteagan* – a day for the worms.'

It was the greatest day of Alasdair's life. The day which measured everything else. Some years later, when he married Katell at St Mary's Star of the Sea, those blue dolphins danced behind the altar. He saw them again the day King George launched the great ship he'd helped to build, the beautiful *Queen Mary*. They were there leaping high into the sky the day he was released from Stalag 383 and that amazing day in 1953 when they were ashore for a week at the Portland Docks and managed to get a ticket for Wembley to see Ferenc Puskas and the Magyar Magicians. And now that he was here, finally retired, with his beloved Katell the dream was coming alive again.

He would have his own boat, just like grandfather once had his. And it would be like Grampa's, though larger. Not ostentatiously so – there was no desire for any of that, but larger so that he could go further out with it, into the deeper waters where the best sea bass could be found. And it would be a thing of beauty too, as well as a joy forever: it would be clinker-built, like the old *sgothan*. A proper thing, not like these modern fibreglass toys. It would move like Ferenc Puskas did that other day. And he had finally persuaded Roderick to sober up long enough to build it, so here we were engaged in the great dream.

It was pure chance that I became involved. I had been going to go to America for that final summer, but the visa fell through at the very last minute so I had decided just to come home instead for one final time. The other guys had all gone their separate ways, and already those university days seemed a long way away, like a different world.

Five of us had shared the flat that final year, behaving like the Famous Five, and now we too were scattered, never to meet again, as I now know. Sheila, who became a doctor and now lives, cared for by her grandchildren, in South Africa. Emily, who was killed in the climbing accident on the Eiger the summer after our graduation. John, who became the famous newspaper editor and personal right-hand man to Rupert Murdoch. Some revolution for the fiery young radical I knew. And Len, who drifted into drugs and who was last heard of heading east to Bangkok just after the war which radicalised us all.

I too had no idea what lay ahead. I had the usual dreams of course – a career in politics, perhaps, or journalism and writing – and no notion whatsoever that I would end up as I am. I don't suppose anyone has. So in many ways that final summer was a kind of last hurrah, or a first paragraph, if only I'd realised. It has, of course, been a limbo in which I have half-resided ever since, and I know full well that here I am again attempting to either break out of – or break into – it. It's my final chance, because honesty too withers with age and custom.

I loved her from the moment I saw her, and that love has never wavered. It has encased every choice I have ever made, and I have never done anything in my life which didn't involve her image somewhere. Her smile has shadowed every other smile; her auburn hair has unjustly covered all others; her freckles have unfairly appeared where they had no right to appear, her eyes been seen when I had no wish to see them. I'm so sorry for it all. For substituting her invisible arm for the arm that embraced me, for touching her untouched arm every time I've loved. Though in my defence I will claim that none of it was ever done falsely, as she now becomes flesh before me in my advancing years, as all things dissolve.

4

NOTHING WAS EVER more solid than the boat we built that summer. We used oak for the floor and fashioned the keel, stem and gunwale from ash. The planks of the boat we shaped from larch, and made the oars from white pine. Old Alasdair insisted on a single mast with uncomplicated rigging, which was basically a large single dipping lug sail that ran along the length of the boat.

It was an absolute joy to watch Big Roderick go about his business. For such a large man he moved with grace, and he handled all the tools and materials with a sensitivity which I can only describe as feminine. He never used brute force or mere strength, but always worked with the grain or through the tool rather than against it. He had little patience with humans, yet seemed to have the love of a saint when it came to handling so-called 'inanimate objects'.

'Everything has a soul,' he kept saying to me, 'and don't believe anyone who argues to the contrary. You don't have a soul – you are a soul. You have a body.'

He'd lift a batten of oak.

'What's this?' he'd ask.

'A batten of oak,' I'd reply.

'Daftie,' he would say. 'Of course it's not. It's the fruit off a tree.' And he would smile. 'By their fruits ye shall know them.'

And he really believed it – not in a daft (his favourite word!)

mystic way, but in a real, practical, down-to-earth fashion.

'Put it this way,' he would say to me when he relaxed at the end of the day's work, 'the world will only treat us as we treat the world. The more we care for it the more it will care for us. The old story, son – we reap what we sow. For what will we eat when we've taken the last herring out of the sea, and the last potato out of the earth? Air? Polluted air?'

And it's remarkable to think now that this was over forty years before folk began talking about global warming. Dear Big Roderick.

He knew fine, of course, that trees and fish and crops and all the rest of it didn't have hearts and souls and minds. What he meant, naturally, was what we're all now recognising, or confessing: that there's a connection between the butterfly and the flood, that it mattered which way natural resources were used and handled.

You could handle a batten of wood with care, or carelessly. You could hammer a nail into a board with brute force or with delicate precision. You could steam and bend a plank patiently and slowly, or do it quickly and harshly with a vice and mallets. Things lasted when done properly. All he did, really, was to treat things with care.

And slowly, I think I began to understand to do the same. To love slowly. Instead of rushing to saw a piece of wood as quickly as possible, I learned to take my time. To select just the right piece from all the pieces that were on offer. To take time in measuring it down to the last centimetre. To make sure that the cut line was completely straight and with the grain and that the bevel edge was exactly as required. Then to take the saw and work slowly through the pencilled line, listening as well as watching. Hearing that urch-urch-urch-urch as the teeth moved solidly across the line as well as seeing that the perpendicular was held, until the unrequired bit sheared off, leaving the perfection. For when the perfect comes, the imperfect disappears.

It was the same when planing the wood. The worst sin of all

was to be irregular and jerky, like a bad fiddler. The aim was to remove the shreds that were unwanted, until only that which was needed remained. Discovering the angel within the marble. The wood makes the boat – not the other way round. Even now in my old age, I still think there is no sweeter sound than the sound of someone planing a piece of wood to perfection and no sweeter sight than watching the sliced shavings curling off the plane on to the floor. And what meaning does any of it have without that smell? Big Roderick's workshop always smelled of wood and citronella and oil, and when I now close my eyes and think of that summer, I can still taste the heady fumes in my nostrils and my mouth waters.

Two things coincided to bring me into boat building for that single summer – Alasdair and Katell lived next door to us, and Big Roderick needed someone to help him. I bumped into him one day in the pub where he stood at the end of the bar drinking water during his sobering-up period.

'I can't just stop like that,' he said. 'I need to wean myself off. A week of water then I'll be right as rain. For six months at least.'

He knew me of course – or at least knew my parents.

'How's your father?' he asked. 'And your mother?'

'Well,' I said. 'Well.'

'The finest fisherman around,' he said. 'And the best nurse. She's saved me a few times.'

He asked me what I was up to, and I said, 'Nothing. Well – nothing much anyway. Just finished uni and...'

He didn't let me finish.

'I could do with a hand. Starting on Alasdair and Katell's boat on Monday, if you're up for a bit of skivvying.'

I told him that I knew nothing about building boats.

'You'll learn,' he said. 'You've got a brain, haven't you?'

And so that's how I started.

Sometimes I got carried away and began to believe that I would do it for a career. What could be better – working with your hands, crafting something beautiful and functional?

Building houses, making haystacks, scything the corn, out in the bogs cutting the peats with a spade. Creating things which would keep you warm and sheltered, which you could handle and use, burn or eat. What could be better than making the boat which you then used to catch the fish which you would then fry to sustain yourself?

To feel the blade of the scythe cold on your hands as you sharpened it with a stone. To feel the wood warm on your hand as you dug the spade deep into the ground. To feel the wet slithery smoothness of the peat turfs as you lifted them out of the bog. The herring scales covering your hands as you gutted them for supper. Though maybe Gaelic aesthetics were different? Maybe here pragmatism mattered more than pleasure, function more than style? Maybe nothing mattered except that which glorified God or served the community: the only things which made life beautiful and useful.

But in my heart of hearts I knew that the job was temporary. Not because Big Roderick would get rid of me or sack me or because there would be no other work once the boat was finished, but because nothing would last. He'd go drinking again, and nothing would happen for months on end, and anyway, was I really fitted for the steady elegance of this kind of work? Could I really see myself in a year or two or ten or twenty still truly believing that literally making things was worth it?

For without belief, nothing mattered. I don't really mean belief in God or in any supernatural deity, but belief in the thing itself, in the thing you were doing, in the boat you were building, in the words you were speaking, in the person you were with, in the language you were writing. I didn't have any of that: only a temporal short-term belief in the value of the thing at the time, in its existential worth. Value might, or might not, come later.

And what a glorious existential reality it was! Lapstraking and tapering and transversing and riveting and clenching and all the rest of it, and the wondrous satisfaction of seeing something you have made becoming what you intended it to be as the keel and the hog and the stem and the apron and the deadwoods and the sternpost and the transom and all the rest of the bits and pieces begin to fit and mould together towards completion.

Though nothing ever is as you really intended, for the garboard is not quite right, and the strakes just not quite as bevelled as you meant them to be, and the keel not quite as balanced as you'd imagined. Even when it finally sailed west on that beautiful blue day, with Alasdair at the halyard and Katell at the tiller, we all knew that it could have been better, that it could have been ever so slightly higher in the water, that the sail could have turned that bit easier, and that it lacked a certain brightness for which we'd striven so hard.

Maybe too hard. No doubt it was what drove Big Roderick to drink and ultimately drove me to this substitutionary life of mine where all these failures are repeated and redeemed in the vain hope that, sometime, words will sing.

You could see the spirit slowly coming upon Big Roderick. He still worked with the same zeal and tenderness, but gradually, day by day a kind of anxiety, which I can only describe as angst, would come upon him through which you could see that he realised – once again – that the boat was not going to be as perfect as he'd hoped, simply because such perfection was impossible.

I tried to reassure him.

'My goodness,' I would say, 'You've made these planks overlap perfectly.'

He would just look at me and say nothing. Or 'aye' if he felt sorry for me. And his work really was perfect: the wood smooth, the rivets flush, the mast a work of art. He too struggled with the same demon: perfection of the life or of the work. And he too was unwilling to refuse the heavenly mansion which I am now building, despite the day's vanity.

The tragedy, of course, was that he actually made no choice, but swayed imperfectly between hope and remorse, sometimes believing that the work – this time round – would be magnificent, but then submitting to the spirit of futility at which point he would, once again, begin sipping the other spirit which would then take him into the graveyard for months on end. At least his struggle was public, unlike mine which was secret and thus more devious and damaging.

And I wasn't even there when he died, finally trapped underground by the demon. I was elsewhere. At the time sitting on a chat show in Canada, pretending to have it all together as I waxed lyrical about 'The Music of Emigration' and about how exiles always inevitably carried their homeland with them in their songs. Abstract guff and rubbish really which earned me a tidy living between the media and various universities which were all fooled into giving me well paid internships in which I gave occasional lectures about the relationship between Gaelic Song and Homeland or – once at a conference in New York – 'The Power of Paradigm in Pre-Millennial Presbyterian Poetry from a Post-colonial Phenomenological Perspective'. I made it all up and received a standing ovation, mostly because I sang the latter half of the lecture in a *canntaireachd* stream which I extemporised and invented as I went along. I thought they understood the joke, but from the conversations afterwards I'm afraid that they all thought it was real. Academics who'd had a humour bypass.

At least Big Roderick knew that that very little of it was, except for the occasional moments when we would all sit and share things round the table. Katell made wonderful *galletes*, as well as *kougin amanns*, which was basically a yeasted dough with butter and sugar to which she added almonds and angelica, folded over into what we would call a crêpe. They tasted wonderful, and were especially good after a salty main course such as lamb and potatoes, which was our staple diet.

Katell herself was a remarkable woman. In many ways she had sacrificed her own life and career to follow Alasdair halfway round the world, but whenever this was implied she would always just say, 'Love is no sacrifice.'

As far as I can now recall, she was born on Armistice Day in

1918, and was thus brought up within sight of Verdun and the Marne, though like all the old people over here she talked very little about it, despite all my efforts. I do know that her father was killed at the front just months before she was born and that her mother, who was a doctor, then remarried an Italian medic who was actively involved in the Resistance when the next war came along. By that time Katell was in Glasgow with Alasdair, who joined the 51st Division just weeks before the invasion of Normandy.

She'd come to Edinburgh in the summer of '35 to study Music at the university, but had run out of money and taken various jobs in the city to survive. 'I gutted fish for a season out at Musselburgh, then got a job cleaning the old bottles at the Royston Lemonade Factory, and then worked in some hotels, scouring floors and making beds.

'But the best job I had,' she always said, 'was as a pianist in the cinema on Leith Walk. They'd play these silent films, twice a night on Wednesday, Thursday and Friday, and five times throughout Saturday and I would accompany the pictures. Some of them of course came with music – the more famous ones, such as the Chaplin ones, but a whole number had no score at all. I especially liked playing to the imported Russian films, when the music could be deep and strong and sonorous!'

Despite her long exile from Brittany and from France, she still retained good traces of her Breton accent by the time I got to know her in the '70s. Invariably, the last syllable of certain words fell rather than rose, which was the local Gaelic tradition. She was, of course, well aware of that and would overemphasise it one way or the other, depending on which one she wanted to mock.

She seemed very old to me at the time, though she was much younger then than I am now, and I regret so much asking her so little, for fear that she wouldn't care to answer. At the time, the gap between youth and age seemed much wider than it is now, and it felt so impolite to begin asking her (this old woman, as I thought) any personal questions over and above what she chose, or happened, to tell me. I didn't know then you had to be as persistent with old people as with young children.

How much I should have asked! But in between the *galettes* and the peat-gathering and the frying of oysters I got a picture of a woman in love. And Alasdair would unconsciously fill in some missing parts, such as the number of wounded soldiers she helped during the war and the occasional times she would still sing, being for years now without a piano or any other musical instrument. I never heard her sing, despite my promptings, though Alasdair once asked Roderick and I to stop working and be still so that we could hear her sing.

We laid down our tools and listened like birds, but nothing came in the wind from down the house, even though old Alasdair stood there beside us, humming the song he was hearing.

'*Domé éspais le jasmin...*' he said. 'Dome made of jasmine...' and he sang for the only time I ever heard him sing, in a confident baritone voice,

> Dome made of jasmine
> Entwined with the rose together
> Both in flower, a fresh morning
> Call us together
> Ah! let us float along
> On the river's current
> On the shining waves
> Our hands reach out...

And he seemed to catch hold of himself, to suddenly become selfconscious saying, 'Ach – a woman's song! But beautiful for all that...' as he walked away back up the hill leaving us to our drilling and hammering.

But it seemed to have been love at first sight: that I gathered. And a love, evidently, which had lasted. I hardly know the details, and they matter little anyway and seem obvious – two young people meet and fall in love and marry. What always intrigued me was the nature of that love, which seemed both natural and reciprocal as if both or either could do what they wanted and whatever they did would please the other. I suppose you could call it freedom, though I think it was more just trust and respect, since freedom is a not a cause but a consequence.

What I sometimes forget as well is that I am of my generation, as they were of theirs, even though they were from two different countries. Wasn't she subservient, I ask myself? Forsaking all for his sake, never the other way round. Who knows what the deal was. No doubt she loved him as much for his weakness as for his strength, for all his folly more than for his wisdom. And who am I to speculate how he loved her? For all I know – and I scarcely know that – are my own failings in the matter. I only know that had I half the peace and contentment they had, I would already have had a heavenly mansion.

I know now that the building of the boat was her final token of love. This was the boat that he'd spoken about that first morning they met in Bruntsfield. She was in what was then called the drawing room, dusting for the lady of the house, when she heard a noise and turned and saw a man dangling from a rope outside the window. He smiled and waved and carried on cleaning the windows as she continued to move inside, polishing the silverware on the sideboard, then dusting down the shelves, then moving towards the window where the piano was. It was a frosty morning, and he made a face on the glass: two round eyes, and a fine nose, and a smiling mouth, and she smiled. Since the lady of the house had gone out visiting, Katell instinctively sat down at the piano and began to play.

Outside the window, Alasdair stopped cleaning and swung on the rope in time to the minuet. They both smiled and laughed. Once she was finished, he rapped on the window, indicating she should open. She did. She pointed to his shoes and he took them off and handed them to her, then leapt in through the opened sash. They stood facing each other, suddenly embarrassed, having nothing to say. Formalities took hold – he stuck out his hand and introduced himself.

'Alasdair,' he said.

'Katell,' she said.

He was immediately charmed by her accent, as she was by his.

'Breton,' she said.

'Hebrides,' he said.

They both stood still, looking round the drawing room. He almost whistled at the extravagance, but checked himself. On the far side, nearest the door, was a huge painting of a ship.

'I like boats,' he said. 'My grandfather had a beautiful boat. One day I'll have a beautiful boat.'

They heard a noise.

'O my God!' she said. 'Out! That's Madame returning.'

She flung him his boots and he swung back out onto his harness and resumed his cleaning. Katell closed the window and began polishing the piano, as the lady of the manor entered. 'Oh,' she said, in her best Edinburgh accent, 'Everyone's busy! And Mister Alasdair's here!' She waved to him through the window, and he gave her a smile and waved the cloth. She left.

Alasdair breathed on the window, which immediately frosted up again. '7pm Fri, Canonmills Clock?' he scratched, backwards. Katell nodded and followed the mistress out.

They were married two months later at the Star of the Sea church in Leith, where the old altar was made out of part of a ship's prow, and then of course the children came, and the move to Glasgow for work and the call-up and the postwar move to Belfast, then on to Liverpool, back north to Burntisland, and on again to Glasgow where he finished as deckhand on the famous Clyde steamer, the *Waverley*. Katell bore ten children, all of whom survived, and by the time I knew her she spoke of twenty-eight grandchildren, eight great-grandsons and 'two darling twin girls who are now six months old and whom I've never seen. They live in Australia.'

Life had prevented the boat from being built. At the beginning, in Leith, they had no money. Working day and night as an apprentice ship's carpenter up there on the Atlantic convoys. Then in Glasgow, as the children came along, they had no time. In Belfast, squashed into an inner-city flat, they had no room, and in Liverpool and Burntisland and then again in Glasgow a million and one other things took priority. Context was all: could he just start building a boat, penniless as they were, in the backyard in Springburn?

Would she, for that matter, start singing an aria from Mozart down at the steamie? Not that ordinary folk would really be bothered, and if they were, so what? But they themselves would be, holding on to the belief that there's a time and a place for everything. Or, as Alasdair himself always said, '*Aig gach nì tha tràth, agus àm aig gach rùn fo nèamh*': to everything there is a season, and a time to every purpose under the heaven. '*Agus b'e sin an t-àm a bhith nam thràill-cosnaidh*': 'and that was the time for me to be wage-slave.'

So the opportunity never really rose until finally, nearing their seventies, they managed to scrape enough together to come back home. At least to Alasdair's, which by then was all the same. Just after they were married a pal at the shipyard gave him a lend of his motorbike which had a sidecar and so Alasdair and Katell finally managed a belated honeymoon, travelling all over Scotland in that rickety contraption.

'We spent most of the time pushing it uphill,' Katell would say, and he would then tell of how they were stopped by a policeman in Stirling as they motored north.

'Do you have a licence?' demanded the officer. 'You realise you need a licence for the passenger as well?'

'But we two are one,' shouted Katell, and the covenant vow sufficed.

So the time and the season had come. The days were hazy with heat. I'd become far too accustomed to the ease of Oxford and it was wonderful to reacquaint myself with the daily sharpness of a Hebridean morning, even in the summer. I'd almost forgotten about the clarity of the light and the way in which the salt air inhabited everything, so that as you woke up you could taste the sea on your lips.

And I'd almost forgotten too how quickly things change. The place was so open and exposed that nothing lasted. One moment the sun would be shining, the next a sheet of rain would sweep in from the Atlantic, which would just as quickly be gone. And as the earth dried, the steam would rise from the ground like a mist. *Ceò* we called it in Gaelic, though there were distinctions to be made between the differing kinds of rain and dew and mist. *Toit* was the smoke from the fire, *driùchd* the dew and *uisge* rain, though my favourites were the ones which contained whole worlds within them, bearing the people's beliefs on their wings.

'*Marbh-laogh a h-Èill Pàdraig,*' Alasdair would say. 'A keen biting wind only felt at the vernal equinox.' '*Fuaradh froise* – that's a strong gust of wind preceding a shower at the time of *Faoilleach*' (January which ran into February). '*Fadag chruaidh,*' he'd say, always looking westwards. 'A fragment of a rainbow which is a sign of bad weather when seen either in the west or in the morning.' '*Breacadh rionnaich air an adhar, 's latha math a màireach* – a mackerel speckling in the sky, a good day tomorrow.' '*Spadag* – a small cloud in an otherwise clear sky.'

Alasdair called a fire not by the common name of *teine*, but by the angelic name of *aingeal*. 'I will not call it *teine* under any circumstances,' he said to me, 'for fire is a dangerous thing, and the flame in the kiln especially so. I always bless the fire that it might cause no harm. And if I say the word *teine* when near a flame, he will come and put the place on fire. The devil needs no encouragement.'

'*Innis dhomh an sgeulachd ud eile a-rithist, mun teine-bhiorach* – tell me that story about the will-o'-the-wisp again,' and he would always at that point light his pipe and send clouds of *toit* into the air.

'There are two versions to it,' he would say. 'The *teine-biorach*, the will-o'-the-wisp, is a *cruth-atharrachadh,* a metamorphosis, undergone by a girl from Benbecula who went to gather the roots of the "rue" at night on the hillocks of the machair. There was a fine imposed on all who did this, as the hillocks would soon crumble in consequence through sand drift. The mother said to the girl as she went off in spite of her counsel, "*Gum bu tig an latha a thilleas tu 's na fuiligte tu bhos 's na fuiligte tu thall*" – "the day will come when you'll come back and you'll neither tolerate being here nor there." Her body was never found except for her *plàd*, her bent-grass bag, and she wanders the earth as a will-o'-the wisp ever since.'

'The other story is that the *teine-biorach* is a blacksmith who lived a bad life and was rejected from heaven and went shivering down to hell but would not be admitted there either as his company was undesirable. He called for an ember of the fire inside to help him warm, and he has been going about with that ember ever since. That's him you see running eternally when you see the will-o'-the-wisp down on the machair.'

'And what was that thing about toothache again?'

He laughed.

'Och that! You don't want to hear that old wife's tale?'

'I do. O, I do,' I protested, and he would tell of the great cure again.

'Well, whenever you get *an dèideadh* – the toothache – what you do is get a good round stone and go to the nearest loch with it. You then fling the stone out as far out into the deepest part of the loch as you can while saying "May I never get toothache again until I see you again." I guarantee that if you throw well and deep you'll never get sore tooth again.'

'And wasn't there another way too?'

'Of course there was – there are always two ways. There are always alternatives.'

He paused, lit his pipe.

'The other way to fix toothache is to clench a bone taken from a grave between the teeth. Any bone picked out of the mould of an open grave will do, but the finger bone of a child is best. It fits better.'

I cycled to work every morning, taking the old cart road which skirted the shoreline. It was that time of year when the earth was ablaze with blossom – the machairs covered in clover and daisies and poppies and forget-me-nots, and – lest I forget – it was also a time when it was still covered with people working. Here and there in ones and twos and threes on their little patches of croftland, some scything the early hay, some harrowing the corn, some planting potatoes. I can still see them in my mind's eye, bent figures in the sun and wind, Lowry-like in the distance. And the bees hummed.

Every day too Alasdair and Katell would keep their eyes on the horizon where they could see the village road from afar, skirting round the sandy beach. Anyone who came or went travelled that single-track road, and so they'd now and again announce, 'That's Donald the Post on the way,' or 'Finlay's van,' or 'Joan's going down to the cockles.'

They kept an eye not because they were nosey, but because they expected one of their children, who'd been travelling though Europe, to appear any day soon. Alasdair would sit there on the bench of wood placed on the old creel, his eyes on the horizon. When the heat haze came he would see mirages: Donald coming back from Woodstock, Andrew returning from Turkey, Elizabeth coming home from Glasgow. Then the shimmer would clarify – an unknown tourist carrying a rucksack, drunken John swaying home with his carry-out, one of the MacNeill sisters on her way to the shop.

And I have the soundtrack for that summer – Joni Mitchell and James Taylor singing to us of their Californian mornings, offering their helping hand. I still attended mass then, and loved the incense rising from the thurible and the lighting and the extinguishing of the candles and the magic moment when the priest unlocked and opened the tabernacle and lifted out the chalice and the gold ciborium. I loved the permanent glow of the votive light and the dazzling vestments the priests wore – the Chasuble and the Alb and the Amice and the Stole and the Cincture – but I especially loved the people, or more exactly, the piety of the people. They honestly believed, and shamed me with their glowing faith. None of it was artificial or showy, and I greatly regret not being one of them, despite all the later revelations which were not in the least their fault. Love cannot be condemned.

It's too easy to blame Oxford, with its wine and dreamy spires and ideas, for far greater men have survived – and thrived – there. Cardinal Newton and the two great Wesleys and George Whitfield, not to mention Tolkien and C.S. Lewis, whose faith was illuminated rather than dimmed at Magdalen and Merton. Their tilley lamps burned brightly like electricity. I have examined myself on the issue, and can find no external assault.

Certainly I came under the influences of the prevailing voices of the time – Ayer was my philosophy tutor and the great pluralist (and atheist) Isaiah Berlin personally supervised my final year thesis – but nevertheless my positions were my own, not theirs. None of them ever suggested that Marx was a better philosopher than Christ (well, pluralists wouldn't, would they?), nor did they argue that Christ was a better politician than Marx. You read or gathered the evidence as best you could and made your own mind up.

So here's the evidence, as speckled and as arbitrary as a hen's egg. Katell kept hens. Dozens of them, ranging free all over the croft. The best layers were the beautiful Rhode Island Reds, with their flash of green feathers in the tail, which laid huge brown eggs that were absolutely delicious. They made wonderful omelettes and soufflés, which were one of Katell's regular specialities. She had a particular way of making them too – not in a pan as was commonplace, but in a proper ramekin, and not in an oven either but over an open peat fire hollowed out in the middle to encase the soufflé as it baked.

Aside from the normal ingredients – unsalted butter, plain flour, milk, goat's cheese, eggs and parmesan – she'd add a whole feast of herbs grown by herself, so that as you tasted the dish you savoured all the above (including the peat flavour!) as well as tarragon, chervil, rosemary and thyme.

Her omelettes were equally delicious, briskly cooked in a very, very hot pan specially made for the purpose by MacGregor's of Inverness, the famous traditional ironmongers, who are sadly no more now either, having gone out of business at the beginning of the millennium.

That's how we made the boat: as part of that summer. It would have been a different boat another summer, for some of us would not have been there then, and it would have been a different boat too had the weather been wet and miserable. As it was, it was built in warmth and sunshine, and I like to imagine that spirit of brightness (despite Big Roderick's reservations) settled round the boat. History, I believe, bears me out.

All through the building of the boat Alasdair wanted to call her *Reul-na-Mara* 2, and in fact I was halfway through making the name board when he changed his mind.

'There can never be a number two,' he declared one day towards the end, as he came up to me from the beach, carrying an oddly shaped piece of driftwood under his arm.

'So I'm going to call her *An Leumadair Gorm – The Blue Dolphin*. I saw a shoal of them jumping once, when I was very young.'

He held up the piece of driftwood which, sure enough, was like a dolphin leaping if you looked at it a certain way.

'See if you can chisel the name onto it for me,' he said. 'I could do it myself, but I never learned how to spell Gaelic properly.'

He looked at me and smiled.

'And make sure it's right.'

5

HELEN SPENT HER whole life searching for the lost fiddle. Not obsessively or even consciously, but she always lived in the hope of seeing it one day, in a pawn shop in Amsterdam, or a village stall in India, or in one of the pit pubs of the Rhonda Valley where she worked latterly as an environmental advisor to the Coal Board.

Strange how things had worked out. In the choice between music and the environment, neither had really won out in the end. That day back in Mull she could have chosen one or the other. They were both on offer.

'So – are you staying?' her mother had asked, once they'd come back in from the orchard. 'You know there's plenty to do here of course.'

She really was without guile, her mother. Straight, honest, desiring nothing but the best. Freckles still adorned her youngish looking face, which remained without any make-up.

'I think... I think, no. I think I'll go back for my year's postgrad.'

It was, of course, really just a way of buying a bit more time, before going out there into the big bad world, before being swallowed up by the big bad wolf. She could still have it both ways for a while yet: music at night and the environmental qualification during the day.

'You can always...' her mother began.

'Yes. Yes of course,' Helen said. 'I know that, Mum.'

She also had a secret love: painting. It had started

innocuously enough. One day she was walking past this secondhand shop when she saw the most extraordinary thing. It was a child's drawing, of little black vertical scratches with lots of churches inside the scratches and a child's peaked black hills on the horizon above the churches. It was, of course, Paul Klee's miniature *Kirchen am Berg – The City of Churches –* and it made a profound impact on young Helen. Could churches – religion – be that frail? And the rectangular blocks round them – were they really blank black canvases?

So she tried her hand at articulating this world, but of course all her early efforts were mere pastiche, very poor imitations of Klee and the other so-called Modernists she came to love. Her scratches were just that, not cosmological truths; her blocks were empty facades without meaning; the relationships between her lines and her circles were false and artificial rather than natural and symbiotic. But she improved. Night classes in drawing skills helped enormously. More night classes in sculpture helped her to understand that everything depended upon everything else. A course in the history of art itself helped her to frame history. But still she lacked that spark. It took almost a lifetime to discover what that spark was. She laid it aside, tossing and turning between music and the environment.

As with all limbos, it was in between uncertainty and assurance, citizened by neutralists and opportunists, halfway between silence and assent. In some ways it was quite a pleasant place, mostly free from any argument or dispute that really mattered, with a splendid view on either side of the glories of heaven and the horrors of hell. A short walk could take you either way, where the best lacked all conviction and the worst writhed with passionate intensity. It seemed quite a safe place, at least in the meantime, until things became a bit clearer. Like having a bath on a chilly day.

She got a part-time job too, in a bar on Sauchiehall Street, which kept all the possibilities open. At weekends she gigged with two different bands, sometimes travelling the country to the various festivals which were being newly established all over the place. She bought a replacement fiddle, though it never truly felt the same: too brittle and bright, lacking the depth and tone of the first, lost instrument.

But it sufficed, and the young people who listened and danced lapped it all up anyway, for it made little difference to them as long as the music was fast and furious and they could laugh and talk and drink and have a good time. And she didn't blame them, for she too was young and free. Who the hell really wanted all that serious stuff anyway, with some poncey critic sitting there musing over whether the A-flat major allegro had a sufficiently determinative quality or whether the subsequent adagio had enough pathos and cathartic passion?

Though she knew now it mattered. That it was the difference between life and death, art and kitsch, heaven and hell, greatness and stupidity – all those mirrors. She'd drifted, and here she was, in consequence, sitting back where she'd started, at Waverley Station waiting for the train westwards. And how different it all was: digital and clean.

She walked over to where the bench had once been which was now the beginning of the direct escalator leading up to Princes Street. For a moment she considered leaping on to the escalator: who knows that she might not find the violin sitting there waiting for her at the top of the stairs? But the information screen and a disembodied voice announced her train and so she passed through the ticket barrier and rolled her suitcase down the platform towards her destination. She sat backwards facing east.

The castle passed, and they went through a tunnel, and stopped at Haymarket. Murrayfield Stadium to the left, PC World to the right. She reversed through Linlithgow and Falkirk and Polmont and Croy and found herself back in Queen Street. Ten paces to the left and she was on the Oban train. This time she sat forward facing, at a table.

She took out her laptop and checked her emails and scanned the news sites and looked out the window as they chugged towards Westerton. How little had really changed: this train still moved slowly, the high rise flats were still there, the Clyde estuary still grey when glimpsed from the bridges. Joe had once said to her that Alf Tupper lived there, behind the garages in Dumbarton.

She'd had a choice. One of the bands wanted to go full-time and she was tempted. A German promoter had signed them up and was offering worldwide gigs on a professional basis – a three-month tour of Japan, as well as some concerts in Singapore and Hong Kong and then some more dates in Australia, and perhaps Canada to follow. The other members of the band pleaded, but she wanted to travel alone for a while without the need for schedules and rehearsals and late night sessions and all the rest of it. She'd done enough of that already throughout her childhood and youth, playing in all the orchestras that were available, touring the Nordic countries and throughout Europe on long overnight bus journeys.

Instead, she saw an advert. One evening after a lecture at the Botanics she saw the advert in a shop window on Byres Road. She must have seen the notice a thousand times before, because she called into the shop most days for her milk and paper and stuff, but it was the first time she read it.

It was nothing startling either: just one of those ordinary vso posters asking young people to volunteer a year of their life to help the poor in the developing world. She noted down the London address and number and phoned the following morning, and a girl said she would send her some information and leaflets and brochures though the post.

She smiled, looking out through the window. How quaint it all seems now! Writing down an address and phone number, then phoning and waiting for a day or two for material to come through the post, in the days before instant access and downloading! Anyway, it came, with details about all the projects they were involved with all over the world. Teaching in Northern Finland, dam construction in Thailand, a thousand and one other projects in Africa and Indonesia and South

America and elsewhere.

They were looking for volunteers to work for up to a year in Peru on a river reclamation scheme alongside the indigenous Yagua Indians in the western Amazon basin near Iquitos. It was the usual global story – loggers and highway builders and oil cartels had plundered the area causing enormous damage to the ecosystem, and the indigenous people in this previously remote district had suffered terrible crop damage and flooding as a direct consequence of unregulated developments. This particular project would involve helping the local population to counteract bank stream-erosion and build up a riparian banking system which would try and restore the river flow to its predevelopment level.

She was there within the month, joining up with a number of other young people from all over the world. The local people, working through the church, welcomed them with open arms and of course in no time at all she knew that the RRSP (the River Reclamation Scheme Project) which she'd seen advertised in the VSO magazine could not be separated from the thousand and one other things which made up the community and which needed to be engaged with, from health to education and justice. The indigenous language needed – or at least ought – to be learnt, to make anything worthwhile.

She stayed with a local family – husband, wife and seven young children – who were a joy to be with. She helped nurse them; she got her mother to post books and toys over for them; she helped teach the mother and the father to read and write. For several weeks she herself fell ill and became completely reliant on them for everything; they encouraged her spirit; they sang to her; they taught her, once she got better, which foods to eat and which to avoid; they taught her how to spin in their traditional manner and how to sow using the shaved-down horn of a cow as a kind of super-needle; they taught her some of their stories and charms and recipes and cures. In turn, once she got better, she helped them to extend their vegetable patch and again got her mother to post over some seedling crops which they tended not to use – including the dry Kerr's Pinks potatoes – which they spat out as inedible.

Gradually, the river itself was buttressed and banked, and with the help of some Swiss engineers an entire water-cleansing filter system was fitted which made it cleaner than it had ever been. The Swiss engineers alongside some Canadian volunteers also introduced an elementary piping system through which clean water, for the first time ever, was actually piped into some of the village homes.

There seemed to be no dispute over which homes along the river delta received this benefit: it was simply chosen arithmetically, with every tenth home, beginning from the hut nearest the riverbank, receiving the blessing. Helen suspected that it would only cause trouble in years to come, but kept quiet about it. Her fear was that every arbitrary tenth house would therefore become more 'valuable' and would set in flow an obnoxious market system in which people would begin to barter for and buy and sell these water-privileged homes.

But that was over forty years ago, and she hadn't been back, so she didn't know. She toyed with the idea right there and then of simply Googling the name of the village and she would instantly know what had happened, but resisted the notion. It seemed, somehow, sacrilegious. It would be like invading the past with a weapon of mass destruction, and for what purpose? Curiosity? Everything had been done in good faith, and hindsight would only add righteousness or regret to it.

Instead, she simply remembered their music. Their basic instruments were the *sutendiu*, which was a kind of flute, and the *chinu* – the drum. But they'd had a fiddle too – a simple little three-stringed instrument which made the most ridiculous sound when played badly – by her – and the most delightful sound when played properly by one of the local musicians. She tried it, of course, and they loved the effort and the ridiculous sound she made, and all the immediate neighbours gathered to share the joy.

Then the local expert, a middle-aged man called Túpac,

raised the instrument and wove magical sounds out of it. His speciality was the *gua* in which he could more or less reproduce the sounds of all the beasts of the forests and the birds of the air through these three strings.

The evening before she left, when the whole community gathered for a feast of maize and yams and sweet potatoes and sugar cane liquor, he played through the night, replicating the sound of a jaguar's growl as the moon rose high over the Andes. She cried that night, certainly. Partially because of the farewell moment, partially because of the sugar cane, but also because of the pure sound of the music which brought dreams to life as they all danced them into existence.

When she returned to Scotland, simply going back to being a gigging musician round the clubs seemed somehow petty and ridiculous. She searched the international pages of *The Times* and *The Guardian* and applied to several organisations which were working worldwide in the environmental sector. They all gave her an interview, and they all offered her jobs, and she finally settled on the Government's own Overseas Agency which dealt with a host of global developmental issues.

Her first posting was, bizarrely she thought, to the Rock of Gibraltar where the British Government was researching the marine ecology of the straits. The particular study was whether the marine biology of the Straits of Gibraltar were significantly different on the two sides of the rock: on the western Atlantic side, and in the eastern Mediterranean side.

They were: there was more evidence of a richer ecosystem in the western stretch, and another study then followed to try and work out the causes, which proved indecisive, some evidence suggesting that the Gulf Stream was the primary beneficial factor, other evidence clearly pointing to the fact that the heavier maritime traffic within the Mediterranean sector led to the inevitably greater pollution.

Helen struggled with the whole thing anyway. Compared to the earthy experience of Peru it was far too abstract, and she knew that a political fudge over the issue was inevitable.

The raw data and the statistics and the analysis would be despatched back to Westminster where it would be swallowed up in the endless bureaucracy of the civil service or ultimately stifled by political posturing and compromise.

After a year there, she was posted to another assignment, this time working in Madagascar on the development of a fruit exporting scheme to Europe. Her job, basically, was to help the local people establish their own networks so that they wouldn't be ripped off by the existing large export merchants who tended to be based in South Africa working through self-appointed agents on the island.

The job was dangerous enough: she was warned off and threatened several times, but through time earned the complete trust of the local people who then ensured her safety. She stayed for five years by which time the fat merchants of Cape Town and Port Elizabeth and Durban were corralled into a twenty per cent share of the market with the main eighty per cent being in the complete control of the indigenous growers and producers.

It was a necessary and useful compromise, meaning that the big merchants still retained an interest, while the locals could use their European and worldwide contacts for brokering some of the deals. In many ways it was the beginning of the Fair Trade movement, though none of the history books have seriously acknowledged the part played in that great development by Helen O'Connor.

Her father, Sean, had been part of the major postwar exodus from Ireland to Scotland in search of work. Arriving initially as an itinerant field labourer, he had travelled the fruit and tattie fields of the Carse of Gowrie and Perthshire, but then found work at the new hydroelectric scheme which had just started at Loch Sloy, then at Cruachan, in Argyll.

Fantastic work – long hours, hard, but with good pay. He lived in a caravan. His great advantage was that he didn't drink, so he was able to save up and after some time bought himself one of the little former railway cottages by Loch Awe.

He met Helen's mother at a dance in Oban. He danced

well, moving with grace and freedom, rather than with any precision. She was up with her family for the summer's holiday from 'down south,' as she put it when he asked her.

'How far south?' he asked.

'South of here,' she replied, and I suppose it was the fun ping-pong of words which first drew them to each other.

'There's a lot of south.'

'And as much north.'

'Ah, but I'm from the west!'

'Which must be east of somewhere…!'

He was from the south himself, of course. County Clare, to be precise – the son of the famous *seann nòs* singer Máire Ní Chonaola, whose father was the fiddler Seosamh Mac Eòin – and though he could sing, and play the fiddle, his own preference was for the squeezebox which he took with him everywhere he went to play parts of the thousands of tunes he knew, though he never left out his favourites, the 'Foggy Dew', the 'Fields of Athenry', the 'Kesh Jig' and the 'Rakes of Kildare'.

'He played beautifully,' her mother said. 'A tiny little red melodeon he called Bridget. Said he liked giving her an occasional squeeze! He was left-handed of course so he'd just play it upside down as it were. Or back to front. "After all," he'd say, "the notes are all the same whichever way you play them. C is C both this way and that." And then he'd move his fingers ever so gently across the buttons and out would come this gorgeous music. As if it had been trapped inside the little box till then, like the fairies.'

Helen stared at her own reflection in the train window. She wasn't that old. Barely sixty, really, which was no age at all these days. He'd hardly been half that age when he drowned, graveless unless you count the ocean as one vast grave west of the Treshnish Isles. She was so young at the time, but old enough to remember it all. 'Oh my God, Oh my God,' she heard her Mum screaming, downstairs, and when she ran down her mother grabbed hold of her and held her tight for such a long time.

His body was never found, which was surprising, as they all believed the tides would bring him ashore at some time in some place between the Ross of Mull and Ardnamurchan Point, but the sea behaved differently, and not once in the fifty years since had a body or bones or a skeleton been found to match his DNA. The world had forgotten too of course, for it was all such a long time ago.

Her mother had a burial place though: the beautiful ancient cemetery of Calaigearaidh with its astonishing view over the Atlantic towards Coll and Tiree and beyond. No one had actually been buried in this old graveyard since the third-quarter of the nineteenth century (one Mary MacDonald, described as a pauper, 1874) but Helen's mother had been friends with old Tomas MacLean who claimed family rights to the two unused lairs in the north-east corner, and willingly agreed that she could have one of them when she died.

'I'll go into the other one myself,' old Tomas said, 'for when I rise I want to be in the company of my own people.'

How strange to be heading home to a place which was not home any more. Hadn't been for such a long time. Though that wasn't true: it was always home, even though her mother was now dead and the house empty and her father lost for so long. Perhaps none of it mattered. Everyone mere pilgrims on earth, moving their tents from glen to street.

She smiled, still seeing the goats on the terrace, the fresh strawberries sitting on the kitchen table, her mother bent double shearing the sheep. She still had the angora cardigan she'd made for her twenty-first. And she'd been back before: it was not that it was some kind of pilgrimage to pay homage to the past. It was only a commonplace journey, to visit some old friends, to place fresh flowers on the grave, to throw some new petals out into the ocean.

That was always the most moving thing: picking the few wild flowers, then going out in old Lachlan's boat, who always turned the engine off and went down below while she unpicked the petals, one by one, and released them into the sea. They would always float and never sink, but eventually drift out of sight in the boat's wake.

This train always missed the last ferry too. So she would spend the night in Oban itself before catching the first boat in the morning. Which is when I saw her again, after all those unknown years.

6

I WOULD HAVE stayed on after building the boat, had I not met Dr Margherita Johnson that night.

The launch had gone really well that morning, and everyone in the whole district had come out to watch the event. I make it sound like the launch of the *QE2*, when of course it was just a little bittie boat which Alasdair and Kate planned to use occasionally for sauntering round the harbour, or – at best – to reach out to Tòrr Point to catch a few cuddies. 'Watch out you don't hit the *Queen Mary*!' someone called. 'To the end of the bay, then hard-a-starboard to New York!' shouted Seonaidh Dubh, who'd spent ten years on the whalers.

Even the English word 'boat' sounds far too grand for the Gaelic word *sgoth*, which really means a skiff. The Gaelic word for boat is *bàta* which signifies a much larger vessel, such as a fishing smack or a cargo boat, though that tends to be a *soitheach* – a ship.

So the skiff was launched, without any great fuss really, except that the local priest was asked to bless the occasion, and having done so everyone then clapped and cheered and had a dram as old Alasdair and Kate climbed into it and rowed away out into the heart of the bay. It was a beautiful early September Saturday morning with hardly a breath of wind in the air, and overhead a clear cloudless sky. The sea was sulphur blue.

We all sat on little hillocks and rocks and drank from cans

of beer and half bottles of whisky and flasks of tea as we watched them throw out the line in the little inlet between the slipway and Clach Oscar, where they were almost certain to have a catch. We had great joy watching them hauling them in, hearing their laughter coming across the bay through the stillness of the morning.

'Time we lit up,' old Archie said, and the few boys and girls left in the village ran off to gather some sticks with which to make the fire. There was a time I'd have gone with them, but I sat where I was sipping from a can of lager. Deborah stood in a polka dot bikini leaning against a tree on the side of the can. The children returned within half an hour or so, each of them with a handful of driftwood, gathered from the shore.

As soon as Alasdair and Kate saw the wisp of smoke rising from the fire they began to row home: within the hour a basketful of fish was roasting on the fire and some singing had begun amongst the women. *Òrain luaidh*, mostly – waulking songs, which rose and fell according to whichever woman decided to lead.

Ancient songs in which many of the words were all mixed up, one minute singing about a tragedy at sea, the next about a love affair on the heath. It didn't really matter, for many of them were extempore in the first place, and often composed afresh in each singing.

The launch occasion lasted until early in the afternoon, when folk began to drift off homewards to attend to other things. Roderick asked me if I'd like to go down to the pub 'for a dram,' but I knew fine what that meant: weeks on end for him on the bevvy, so I declined.

He'd enter the fairy knoll anyway, whether I accepted or refused. But I took a lift with him back home as far as the pub road end, flinging my bicycle into the back of his pick-up van.

'So,' he said, as he pulled into the lay-by at the road end, leaving his engine running. 'That's it then. We'll see you around?'

'Yes – yes of course,' I replied. 'Any time you want a hand, just call in. I'll be more than willing to learn.'

It was the last time I ever saw him.

I cycled home and decided to go for a walk down on the machair later that evening, after tea. I took the old river path which skirted the disused mill and eventually reached the sea via Loch an Eilean.

The ruins of all the old thatched houses lay on the east side of the loch and I paused there for a while before climbing the rocks which served as a short cut to the machair itself. As I neared the top I heard a shout to my left and looked over towards the abandoned sheep fank, where someone was standing on top of the old stone wall, beckoning to me.

I walked over and could clearly see the nearer I came that it was a photographer.

'Sorry for shouting at you,' she said, 'but you're the first person I've seen down here for hours. The light is just perfect right now, and I thought...'

'You could do with a prop?' I asked. 'A human prop, as it were?'

At least she had the grace to smile.

'I'm afraid I'm not much of a crofter to pose amidst these ruins for you,' I said. 'I'm only a pretend native. Just a student, really.'

'That's all right,' she said, 'because I'm just a sort of pretend photographer. Only joking – what I really need anyway is the silhouette of a figure against the old disused fank.'

I got it. The usual stuff. Some fancy photographer visiting the peasants to do art. Fragments against the ruins: emptiness against emptiness. I decided to be equally facetious.

'It'll cost you,' I said. 'Five pounds for every snap.'

To my surprise, she agreed. Well, not quite in that way, but she did say,

'Don't worry. If any of them are used professionally, you will be paid. The *National Geographic* always honour their contracts.'

'Ah!' I said to myself. 'The good old NG.'

'What's the commission?' I asked her.

She looked down at me from the shoogly stone wall.

'The commission is called "From the Lone Shieling".'

'Where would you like me to stand?' I asked.

'There,' she said. 'Right where you are.'

'Right here? At the centre of the universe, as the old fool put it?'

'So,' I asked her afterwards as we walked back across the moorland to her car, 'you just came today?'

'Yes. Just this morning.'

'And why didn't you bring your own silhouette with you? Or at least arrange one beforehand? We do have telephones, you know.'

'They're always best done impromptu. Setting everything up always ruins it.'

'Bare ruined choirs?'

She asked me if I'd like a lift and I said no – that I was going for a walk down the machair. 'You can join me if you like,' I said. 'As long as you leave your camera in the car.'

She hesitated.

'Don't worry,' I added. 'No one will steal it. Especially if you leave the car open.'

We walked down through the village and I could of course sense the murmurings behind the curtains.

'Isn't that…?'

'Yes – yes, of course it is, but who's that woman with him?'

'I don't think she belongs here. No, I don't think I've ever seen her before.'

'Och, she'll be one of his university friends, home on holidays.'

We passed the last house in the village, which also doubled as the local shop, and walked round the edge of the Bull Field which brought us to the shingle road west. The gate was tied with wire fencing so we climbed over it and walked down through the sand by the cornfields which had just been harvested that very day. You could still smell the fresh hay gathered in the remaining stooks which would be taken home the following week.

'An interesting job, then?' I ventured. 'The Hebrides one month, Hawaii the next?'

'Wonderful,' she said. 'Couldn't be better. But I'd really rather not talk about my job. Look at that building over there. What is it?'

'The old seaweed factory.'

'Mmm.'

We walked over towards it. A couple of old lorries stood rusting in the yard, and the doors to the former drying kilns were wide open.

'About twenty locals worked here until it closed a few months ago. I don't really know why it shut – I suspect artificial fertilisers are more economical.'

We moved down past the factory on to the sandy beach. It stretched for miles both to the north and the south and was completely empty. The evening sun was settling over Orasay.

I hesitated.

'Your name – Margherita. It's not – common.'

'No, I don't suppose so. It means daisy. Italian. My grandfather was from Naples.'

'It would be Mairead in Gaelic. That means pearl.'

'Just call me Daisy.'

We walked, aimlessly enough, for there was nothing to aim for or at. Sometimes together, sometimes she would head off down towards the sea's edge and pick up a pebble or a shell or a wisp of seaweed, sometimes I would climb up on to the marram strand where all kinds of debris had been washed ashore – corks, old bottles, bits of plastic, canisters of oil, dozens of buoys. Seonaidh Beag would already have gone off with anything valuable. He was always there at sunrise. Once he found a watch inside a metal box: a diamond-studded Rolex which worked as well as the day it was made.

We walked north towards the old settlements next to

the Bronze Age roundhouses. Up little dunes and down into sandy hollows. Like running in and out of your mother's arms. No wonder the little people stayed here, completely safe underground, dancing and playing and making music. Their little round houses were so simple. The door facing East where the sun rose every morning as it does now right there over Ben Mòr. And daily they moved *deiseil* – clockwise – from kitchen to living area to sleeping quarters to death chamber in the space between sunset and sunrise which never saw any light. Each day they moved that way, sunwise, from morning till night, from birth to death.

We eventually sat on a small grassy knoll at the edge of the machair looking south towards Barra.

'What else have you planned?' I asked. 'While you're here.'

'The assignment is for a week. I spent two days in Lewis, a day in Harris, and now here. I fly off on Tuesday morning. The reporter was here two months ago. He gave me a list of things to photograph, and I'm just going through them, meticulously, one by one. Sheep, cattle, eagles, fishing boats, stark Protestant churches, pretty Catholic ones, Marian shrines, empty shielings, single-track roads, old tractors, bicycles, close-ups of marram grass, water lilies, and of course people. The older and more weather-beaten, the better.'

'And fanks with silhouettes?' I asked.

She laughed. 'I got bored. Humanity always makes stone and grass more interesting.'

We walked back.

'Maybe I could give you a hand while you're here over the next couple of days? I know all the places, and the people, around here so could make it just that bit easier for you?'

She agreed, and indeed it did make things much simpler for her in many ways – I took her to see Dr John, the local ornithologist, who led her through the bird sanctuary, and to see Fr Iain who posed with all the golden chalices for her, and young Angus MacDonald who had the best fishing boat in the area and who was pleased to take her out for some lobster-creel shots, and to see a hundred-year-old Peggy in her thatched cottage. Their photographs later adorned the magazine, despite the list that the Washington reporter had given her earlier.

And we got to know each other better. I was infatuated with her: she was beautiful, smart and elusive, though she made it pretty clear that she was not attracted to me in that way.

'I like you,' she said. 'You'll need to do something with your life.'

And I wasn't offended at her counsel, partially because I lived in hope. You never know. If you hang in there, all kinds of strange and wonderful things can happen. Miracles can develop like photographs. Look at Deirdre and Naoise, and how initial separation ultimately led to passionate love. Saint Paul hated Christ and came to love him. But that was only after the Damascus road. Can you learn to love?

'No,' she said. 'It takes a miracle.'

I dared to ask her, for I had nothing to lose. Though I asked it as a kind of joke –

'What then? What do think I should "do with my life"'?

She answered without any irony, as far as I could make out.

'Leave here. Come with me to London. Get yourself a job. Live. Then you can come back here if you want.'

'When I am old and grey and full of sleep…?' I suggested.

'Please yourself,' she said.

So I took her advice. She left me her card when she flew off on the Tuesday.

DR MARGHERITA JOHNSON
PHOTOGRAPHER, CHELSEA

'Phone me when you get to London,' she said.

I did. She came out to meet me at Heathrow and we got the train back into town.

'Not so many silhouettes here?'

'More than you'd care to imagine.'

She had a spare room, so I boarded there for a while. I think that suited her too for she was so often away on assignments, and it was maybe safer for her flat. She even got me a part-time job as an art technician where she occasionally taught herself, at the Slade School of Art.

My initial job was to prepare and mix clays for the students, and to make sure that the photographic and other equipment were in working order. A mere matter of ensuring that there was sufficient paper and enough chemicals in the darkroom, and plenty bags of clay in the sculpture workshops.

Margherita herself was a Visiting Professor at the Slade and held occasional seminars not only on the techniques of photography but also on the sociology of the art. She persuaded me to send in my CV and argue the case for modules to be taught on The Art of Indigenous Cultures, and I must have been quite convincing in my presentations for they agreed to start a series of lectures in which I taught that it was important – in these emerging post-colonial times – to understand the indigenous non-imperial art of this nation.

I argued that Visual Art (with a capital A) had been perceived and presented in the United Kingdom as the art of the canvas and the gallery, and as the sculpture of the exhibition and the garden, which by definition made it a class-based Art, by simple virtue of the fact that it was only the moneyed classes who had access to these facilities. As a consequence, I suggested, the art of the poor was ignored and marginalised, and an essential part of that mistreatment was the complete disregard for the indigenous art of England, Ireland, Scotland and Wales. I waxed lyrical about the Scottish Gaelic example, presenting myself as an expert on something I really knew very little about, but it convinced many and as I said earlier, kept me in well paid if dishonest employment for decades. 'Our stories were our canvas,' I pompously declared.

I had one particular theory which sounded so plausible that even I believed it: which is that Scottish Presbyterianism was essentially a visual art as great as that of the Roman Catholic Michelangelo (and Fra Angelico and all the rest of them) except that it was imagined and expressed through their often austere prayers rather than on canvas or on cathedral ceilings. I thus argued that if we were to even begin to understand the history of art in European culture we needed to completely liberate the parameters of academic discourse, to include sermons, prayers and psalms. It convinced many, and within five years I too became as Margherita, a Doctor of Philosophy.

By that time, I'd long separated from her. We had our moments. We tried. We really did. Or at least I did. She'd been away in North Africa and came back in great spirits, having spent three months travelling with, and photographing, the Yahia Bedouin tribe of eastern Morocco. I went out to the airport to meet her. She looked absolutely wonderful: glowing with health which somehow contrasted so vividly with the sun-baked tan of those returning on the holiday flights.

We made love for the first time that night, and that too was wonderful. Nothing seemed artificial as we lay there afterwards, smoking and talking. They really were wonderful cigarettes she'd brought back from Marrakech. I was convinced they were laced with marijuana, but she assured me they weren't, and I believed her.

'No, no, no no,' she said. 'I saw the man himself, Attayak Ali, making them and rolling them. Just pure black Moroccan tobacco. The spiced coconut oil is what gives it the zing.'

We had some great times together, made all the sweeter, I think, by our knowledge that it wouldn't last. Without getting too soppy about it, like one of those lovely sunsets you enjoy simply because you know it's unrepeatable, and not because it won't be happening like that again the following night but because you know you won't be there then, you'll have caught a flight home, or driven on to the next town, or caught the bus or train back home. You linger, of course, and stretch it all out and open another can of beer on the beach and add a bit more wood to the fire, but once the sun has gone down a melancholy settles too, despite all your efforts at extending the joy. Then folk drift off, and wander away, and the barbecue fire is left to fizzle out as darkness settles.

I try and picture her in the darkness. And I can't fully recall anything. The shape of her mouth or the colour of her eyes or the incline of her jaw or her height or voice or posture. She was tall and lithe and desirable and moved gracefully and laughed raucously and was full of life but the details are all insubstantial. Maybe they don't really matter, though I remember how much it mattered then that her cheekbones were so finely chiselled and her figure so sensual. All I remember now is our joy at being young and alive.

We split without much acrimony, and I would see her occasionally and have coffee with her and catch up with things, since I'd moved not that far away – to Parsons Green. I continued my evening lecturing at Slade, and subsidised that with a day job in the White Horse bar. There I daily served a crowd of civil servants and through time they suggested I join the service. The exam was easy enough and with my drinking friends opening some doors I was able to join the diplomatic wing, first of all as a junior assistant in the Foreign and Commonwealth Office (the FCO) and then as a senior officer in the visa and immigration service. This basically consisted of dealing with visa applications and entry clearance procedures, which bored me to death even though my posting was in Copenhagen.

I resigned on a whim and returned to London where I rented a room in Greenwich. Here I was at the centre of the universe. My parents used to listen to the Shipping Forecast. Tyne, Dogger, Fisher, German Bight. Imminent. My mother never liked the word. She had three brothers, all drowned in a storm while out fishing. Greenwich Mean Time. The world is measured from here. Longitude 0°. I visited the observatory, of course. Stood on the famous Meridian Line, one foot in the eastern hemisphere, one foot in the western. A guide led us round. 'Every place on Earth is measured in terms of its distance east or west of this line,' he said. The building itself is very beautiful. Wren's. Imagine having built this and St Paul's. I bought a postcard which said 'The centre of world time.' I intended sending it to my parents, but couldn't bear the lie, so I wrote it out for Margherita, but never sent it.

I went down to the docks instead. Maybe I should add that this was all before the Thames changed into a housing market. St Katherine's Dock was still in full swing and as I passed the London Seamanship College I looked at the poster in their window. 'A Career at Sea' it said at the top and, in smaller letters at the bottom, beneath the beautiful picture of a ship berthed in a bay beneath a cloudless sky, 'Mount Fujiyama on a June morning'. I entered the building and asked the woman at reception for more information and she gave me a pile of brochures and entry forms about the Merchant Navy, which I took home with me.

There were several options: catering, deckwork, navigation and engineering. I studied the navigation requirements, filled in the forms, and sent them off. I received the letter the following Saturday, asking me to report out to the Sea Training College at Gravesend on the Monday. It was one of those sultry London days. Even the Thames had a bit of colour as if the sun had managed to squeeze something blue out of the slime. The college was still in the beautiful old Gothic building at Chalk Marshes. Despite the heat outside, the huge rooms inside were chilly.

A shoe-polishing machine stood in the corner of the ground floor. I went over and stood there listening to the whirring and the swishing until my shoes shone like a gilded mirror. I could never pass one of these machines from then on without sprucing myself up. Tragically, they have now gone out of fashion. I was led up to the top floor where a man wearing a beautifully tailored captain's outfit sat behind the desk. He was in his shirt-sleeves, with his cap on the table.

I failed at the first hurdle. He studied the form I'd filled in, then showed me a circular chart and handed me enormous black spectacles. He asked me to put the glasses on and said, 'Just tell me what colour you see.'

I looked at the chart. 'Red,' I said.

He flipped the chart, clockwise.

'Blue,' I said. 'Yellow. Orange. Green. Indigo. Purple.'

He put the chart down once I'd taken my glasses off. 'Sorry,' he said. 'Colour blind. It needs to be perfect before acceptance. Sorry to have taken you so far out of your way.' He stood up and stretched out his hand. 'Best of luck. Maybe you could try the police?'

On the way back, I experimented looking out the bus window. A red roof. *Dearg*, I said to myself. Red. Maybe that was the problem: perhaps my own language had a different colour code. A woman wearing a beautiful blue coat walked down the street. Wearing a *còta liath*. A children's slide in the playpark was *buidhe*. Yellow. The lights turned orange. I smiled. No – we had no real word for that. No 'proper' word, if you like. Just *orains*, evidently from the English. *Ruadh*. That was the word for it. That's what Alasdair would have used. '*An Abhainn Ruadh*', he would say – the rusty river. For what function did orange have in that world where the fruit was non-existent, and the traffic lights still to come. *Uaine* was green, though that too was relatively new. It used to be called *glas*, which folk now translated as grey. So, in the old days, green grass would be *feur glas*, which now literally meant grey grass. Perhaps I wasn't colour blind at all; maybe just had a different colour chart.

It seems like yesterday. I can stretch out my hand and feel the starch in his shirt which left it so beautiful and uncreased, with the exquisite Nelson Loop on the shoulder. And I remember the insignia on his cap, a small golden anchor inside the red oval within the golden wreath of oak leaves. I can remember the faint aroma of tobacco from him, and the way he stood at the high arched window looking down as I left the building.

So I never went to sea. Instead, for reasons that are now so imprecise compared with the detail of that single day, I finished up teaching. I now wonder about that man. What precision – or imprecision – had left him on the top floor of that building that hot summer's day? I like to think that he too had followed a whim, and one day seen a poster and not being colour blind had ended up seeing the seven wonders of the world, including the sun rising over Mount Fujiyama on a June morning.

If I had my chance all over again, I would ask him all that: about Rio in the spring, and the Gulf of Mexico in a storm, and sailing through the Suez Canal before the time of the blockade. But he would have looked at me with those clear blue eyes and answered factually, when I wanted to hear about the poetry and the fear of it all. Like me, I don't suppose he ever told that to anyone.

When I first started teaching I rented a balcony flat which I then bought once I married Marion. An old Russian lady lived downstairs, and when she decided to move in with her son in St John's Wood, we managed between us to buy her apartment, which gave us a nice three-bedroomed flat in that very pleasant area of London. As a free gift she left us her Venetian vase.

Marion was from York, though her family had also originally been Scottish, but that was way back in the late eighteenth century. She was a lecturer too, but in a very different discipline from mine – Microbiology.

She taught the subject at King's College, and if nothing else brought me to a much healthier lifestyle once I realised the full health implications of what I was eating and drinking and smoking! I met her at a trans-college conference in the city where all the differing academic departments had (for once) come together to take a united stand against central government cutbacks in education. And that was even before the blessed Margaret Thatcher came to power! I think it was in the days of Ted Heath, though if I remember correctly, all the protests were directed at Keith Joseph.

We had a very pleasant marriage, marred only by the fact that we were unable to have children. We discussed IVF and all the other options, of course. Having an inhouse expert, as it were, saved lots of time and hassle, and money too no doubt, and we pretty quickly decided to leave things as they were and just concentrate on our careers without bringing too many sought complications our way. I'm not sure that decision greatly helped our careers, but let's put it this way – I don't suppose it did any harm.

My own post was extended first of all to being full-time, then to the actual establishment of a small department in which I was initially Acting Head before being appointed Head and Professor of what proved to be a popular and expanding department. By the time I took early retirement we had a full department quota of twenty full-time and fifteen part-time staff with a student roll of well over a hundred, not counting the part-time and pathway students from other disciplines. It's not an erotic poem, but it paid me well.

There was a particular growth in the number of overseas students we attracted to Slade's and my greatest joy these past years was in overseeing the development of the Overseas Exchange Programme, which saw researchers and teachers and students from over a hundred indigenous cultures involved in sharing their perspectives on native art with each other.

I managed to combine this somewhat busy career with media interests too, which brought further travel my way. I started with a weekly column about Art in the *Evening Standard*, which was soon syndicated to many of the other major evening papers in the big cities, and of course through that I was inevitably invited to a whole host of conferences, which led to some contracts for editing and publishing some books about indigenous art until – and I don't know how it really happened – I came latterly to be considered the worldwide expert on the subject. It was all interpretation as in the old days when you were given a poem and asked to define what the poet meant. As if you could define anything.

A *mùdag* is a wickerwork little creel all closed in, but with one little opening on one side to admit the hand, and is used for keeping teased wool. It is in shape oval like a rugby ball and about twice as bulky. How can one little word mean so many others? A *coileach* is a black cockerel hatched in March which has more power for terrifying goblins by his crow than a cockerel hatched in autumn. Which is why a black cockerel is considered a lucky bird to have about one's house. Though that same word, *coileach*, also means peaked waves and a choppy sea when the wind and the current are against one another.

In school we used to have Poems for Interpretation.

I wandered lonely as a cloud that floats on high o'er vales and hills, when all at once I saw a crowd, a host, of golden daffodils; beside the lake, beneath the trees, fluttering and dancing in the breeze. Continuous as the stars that shine and twinkle on the milky way, they stretched in neverending line along the margin of a bay: ten thousand saw I at a glance, tossing their heads in sprightly dance. The waves beside them danced; but they outdid the sparkling waves in glee: a poet could not but be gay, in such a jocund company: I gazed and gazed – but little thought what wealth the show to me had brought: for oft, when on my couch I lie in vacant or in pensive mood, they flash upon that inward eye which is the bliss of solitude; and then my heart with pleasure fills, and dances with the daffodils.

ANSWER EACH OF THE FOLLOWING QUESTIONS TO THE
BEST OF YOUR ABILITY:

1. The title of the poem is... (1 mark)
2. It was written by... (1 mark)
3. What is the basic situation? (2 marks)
4.   Are there conflicts in the poem? If so, what are they?
    (3 marks)

I have of course also sat on a number of boards and government trusts and committees which have discussed the future direction of art in this country, and count people such as former Prime Ministers John Major and Tony Blair and some other world leaders in my circle of friends. Sorry to make all this sound rather boastful – it's not meant to be. It's just a quick résumé of my career: its worst fault, I suspect, is that it is leaden, and sounds like a job application with a CV! The years have taken their toll, and destroyed spontaneity.

Marion's career was no less 'successful,' if you want to use that word. She too progressed to being Head of Department (specialising herself in Parasitology), but then moved sideways into college management, ending up as Principal, a post she carried out as a duty rather than as a vocation.

'It's critical for the wellbeing of the institution,' she argued. 'I know full well it means endless long boring meetings, and often huge compromises, but someone's got to do it, and I firmly believe that in the long run it will be for the benefit of all the students.'

So she sacrificed herself for them, even though it killed her in the end.

I'm so tired. God, am I tired. Is that belief? To call upon the name. How did it all happen? So quickly too. I occasionally remember my name, as it was then. Alasdair. Alexander in English. Sometimes shortened to Sandy. Some people called me Alex. How my mother always put the emphasis on the first two letters, so that the rest of my name always sounded like a question left hanging. Al so strongly put, then the asdair as if some kind of resignation was setting in. I called myself that for a while. Aly. Big Al they called me. And Ali Mohammed used to come round the houses every spring with a large magic case full of clothes. When he opened it, no one could believe the amount that was inside: vests, pants, shirts, trousers, jerseys, caps, handkerchiefs, stockings and all kinds of secret wonders that only my mother was allowed to see. Ali carried his case strapped to his back on his bike, so how come it was always newly full to the brim at every house, no matter how many things people bought?

I lie awake thinking of the speed at which everything happened. First of all slowly, really slowly, like a slow motion film. We used to make *bàtachan- seileasdair.* Iris boats. Boats made out of irises. The best of them were found down by the rock pool next to the stream. You plucked one, then cut your way through the sheaf with your teeth, then looped the sharp end of the iris back into the hole you'd made and there you had it: abracadabra my bonny lies over the ocean the big ship sails on the ally-ally-oh, an iris boat that would take you all the way across the Atlantic to America itself.

The best place to launch it from was the old bridge by the ruin. You could stand on the flat stone which held the bottom of the bridge and release your boat and the game was then to run as fast as you could up the slope by the side of the bridge and get to the other side in time to catch it just emerging down below. It all depended. If it had been raining heavily and the stream was running fast, you had no chance: by the time you reached the bridge your *seileasdair* would be somersaulting away through the rapids down the other side. The other major hazard were the stones which bedded the stream – if the weather had been too dry and the water was low, likely as not your boat would wedge between the rocks and make the game impossible. The dream was always circumstantial: to find the right kind of iris, to make the right kind of cut with your teeth, to loop back the stem perfectly, to find the river running free. When the word became flesh you believed and watched in awe as it flew from your hands, landed like a seaplane in the water, glided between the rocks as you ran and then waited for you as you leant over the parapet, where it would emerge out into the sunlight, very much like the *Queen Mary* herself, blowing her horn at the Statue of Liberty.

Age is a dreamy process. I'm forever now taking little nods where time dissolves, and the strange thing is that it is always quiet when I waken. I drift off in the early afternoon while the birds sing outside the window and someone mows a lawn in the distance, and sometimes I hear a shout or two, and then I'm once again rolling a marble down the rock which lay between the river and the byre. You had to climb it from the far side and sit on the very top from where a long sinewy crevice ran all the way to the bottom. If you released the marble too quickly it would spill out of the crevice, but if you were careful and lay face down on top of the rock and stretched yourself full out the marble would then hold the hollow at the top for a moment or two before running all the way down the crevice to the grassy bottom. It moved right and then left and then straight down, then to the right again and then in a long slow sweep down to the left where it would nestle safely in the grass. The trick was to do it as fast as you could without the marble spilling out, and I once managed to do it to the count of ten.

And every time I waken there is that soft, distant hum and I wait to hear voices and none come. 'Alasdair?' she would shout. 'Alasdair?' And the voice is not there. Or there would be the sound of a ball hitting a home made cricket bat, or the sound of Catherine playing with her dollies, or the lowing of a cow far away, and there is silence. I listen and I can hear the grass grow.

Her breathing has become light. Almost indistinct. Faint. I didn't think anything was ever faint before. Even on the calmest of summer days, something would be moving. Clouds. Bees over the clover. The bog cotton on the moor. Seonaidh Dhòmhnaill Alasdair or Seasag Ruairidh Sheumais with a stick herding the cow. And there was always noise. Geese, ducks, hens, dogs, boats. The priest's car. The minister's car. The teacher's car. The travelling shop-van. MacBrayne's bus. A plane high up in the heavens and the peewit crying on a spring morning.

Maybe the moon was nearest to this state. Late autumn, once the harvest was home, was moon-time. The full moon on the 23rd of September. It was a Thursday. The haystacks were all secure in the yard. Coming back from the machair I saw the geese going south. The moon rose over Easabhail. *Bha i ruadh*. She was red. *Gealach an Abachaidh*. The harvest moon. Nothing moved. Not even the sea could be heard. It cast a faint light on all the earth. Like this. So that the rocks and the stream and our house and even the huge church on the hill became small. Even if I stood on top of the highest hill and reached right up on tiptoe and had a long stick in my hand I wouldn't be able to reach the moon. She was too far away. For the moon is feminine. As is the sun. The earth is masculine. The sea is both.

Our neighbour could be in two places at once. He was called Mìcheal, and not only had the gift of second sight but was also sometimes taken away by the Host of the Dead. They would come for him at twilight through the small western window and transport him south west east north for days on end to distant places. The Host were led by Niall Sgròb and Mìcheal told me that they had taken him across the great ocean to a place which was twinkling with lights. I asked him how they had carried him. 'By the hand,' he said, 'like you would take a child.'

As a child, I too could be in two places at once. I remember once when I was walking across the moor with my mother I ran on ahead and when I looked back I could see the two of us walking towards me. And it worked not only looking back. Another day I was scything the hay with my father when I looked across into the next field where I was sitting holding his hand. I now regret that there are two places.

I hold hers now. A strong hold. Weak. A hold like the one I held when I put the ring on her finger. Thumb. Index. Middle. Wedding. Pinky. A gold ring. That's now too big. A hand I held in Cornwall and in St Tropez when we were on our honeymoon. Honey. Moon. I do. Yes, and I will, yes I do, yes and yes and yes and yes, breathed Molly Bloom.

No no no no, as dear Margherita said, in better times. I read of her occasionally too from her recluse in New Mexico. What a beautiful, honest, and straightforward woman. As was Marion. I don't want my... my regret... to diminish her, for she too was straightforward and honourable. She was always ready to forgive and, like all of us, naturally assumed that the world was made in her image. She found it so genuinely distressing therefore to encounter colleagues who were unforgiving, bearing little grudges forever as if they could improve on Sisyphus. She was okay, okay? And none of it is self-pity. Whatever else, o God, save me from that.

There is a morning time when I waken, just before dawn, and I'm back there. It's warm, and there's a kind of soft humming sound in the distance, and bicycle clips being put on, and an oven door closing or opening. It clicks when it closes and clucks when it opens. And the smell of newly baked scones on the *greideal*, the griddle, and once we have these, we'll walk north, I think, to Roghasdail to see if the boys would like a game.

I'm so glad my Dad fixed the ball yesterday: you'd hardly know the leather had been sown. If I play at outside-left it will be best on that machair slope, 'cause I know the inclines and hollows so well. My eldest sister is singing, and even I know the words by now: it's now or never, come hold me tight, kiss me my darling, be mine tonight. And I realise it's London, and now, and that I will never see them again.

I'm so tired. God, am I tired.

And then I remembered her. Just like that, out of the blue as it were, for no apparent reason, as I sat at an outdoor table in a café in Paris in the September sunshine. The *Rue de Richelieu* where I often went in the mornings for my double shot of espresso: an old habit which I'd allowed to creep back in following Marion's death.

That and the occasional Gauloise and the glass of vintage red in the evenings. My friend Doctor Jacques, with whom I often played chess, assured me it was the best thing in the world.

'Not only good for your heart, but even better for the spirit! *Santé*!'

We'd always talked of relocating to Paris and never gotten round to it, but during her long illness we persuaded ourselves to move there, maybe finally permitting ourselves some liberty.

The house in St John's Wood sold for an absolute fortune and allowed us to buy a beautiful small *maison de ville* in the lovely sixth arrondissement, by the Jardin du Luxembourg, where I used to wheel her round the ponds every day. She was brave throughout the whole thing, and it was some relief to us that we were able to share simple things in the final days to make life's long sacrifice worthwhile.

They used to hold little toy yacht races on the Luxemburg ponds, and the grown-up men who played these games with such fierce competitiveness in these end days gave us a special welcome and would insist that Marion be brought right into the heart of the action, and would help push the wheelchair down to the water's edge where she could watch the yachts racing across the water from close quarters. I knew she especially loved the old boys' shouts and cries as they urged their beautiful little motorboats across the pond – *Mon Dieu! Sacre bleu! J'en ai morre! C'est dans la poche!*, shouts as if victory or defeat meant life or death to them which they then resolved with hearty backslapping hugs to each other when it was all over.

And I suddenly remembered her, pausing briefly on the stairs as she climbed and I descended the stairs between the deck and the restaurant.

'Sorry,' I remembered saying to her, trying to stand to one side, and how she smiled and said,

'O, don't worry – I'll get by.'

I wanted to touch her arm as she passed, but I stayed my hand and she left. The *rue de Richelieu* was filling up with office and shop workers arriving for their lunch, and as I rose to my feet I could smell the jasmine from the street vendor passing riding by on his bicycle, carrying home a splendid bouquet on his saddlebag, for his wife or lover.

7

ALASDAIR AND KATE had the time of their lives with the boat. Not only on that great day of the launch, but every day after, whether the boat was in the water or not. All through that fine September and equally fine October, they were out in it almost every day. It was one of those rare autumns which brought long sun and clear winds, and few gales and rain, so that whichever way they went they found safe shelter and a good catch of fish.

'*Foghar gu Nollaig, Is Geamhradh gu Fèill Pàdraig; Earrach gu Fèill Peadair; Samhradh gu Fèill Màrtainn.*' autumn to Christmas; winter to St Patrick's Day; spring to St Peter's Day; summer to Martinmas, was how old Alasdair still portioned the year. And when the yellow moon of Michaelmas came and went, he began to prepare to take the boat ashore. By the time Hallowmas came, the skiff was secure in the old byre, which he'd opened up from the south gable.

The long winter was spent caring for the boat: cleaning those parts which had already begun to soil, which had scraped and scratched here and there as they fished, and adding lovely little extras which neither Big Roderick or I had time or mind to fix on at the time.

He cushioned the gunwale, scraped down and repainted the hull, welded new holdings to the keel, smoothed off the garboard, tightened the clinchers and aprons, and spent a good deal of time too on the anchor itself, which most other seamen tended to ignore. It shone, as did the boat itself by the time spring came with its steady winds.

They relaunched her on St Patrick's Day, in a squall which suddenly blew up from the west. 'I should have known better,' he muttered. '*Reothairt na Fèill Moire 's boille na Fèill Pàdraig* – The springtide of Lady Day and the fury of St Patrick's.'

But nevertheless he had to balance things out: to cope with that fury or to risk things with the greater danger of not putting the wood into water until after St Patrick's Day, which was certainly to anger the fates. He knew fine that some cheated, and would just sprinkle the wood with water if the weather was too rough on St Patrick's Day, but Alasdair thought any god worth his salt would look with disdain at such a notion. Either face the storm, or deny it all. Surely the deities didn't trade in compromises and deals?

He treated himself to a smile when the sudden squall passed, leaving the sea blue and still as far as the eye could see. The quieting of the storm. Kate took to the oars and they moved north-eastwards towards *Bàgh an Dùin Mhòir* where the cockle-strand lay. They anchored the boat there in shallow waters and waded to the shore, buckets in hand.

The tide was just right: ebbing, and leaving enough visibility into the sand to see the razorfish. You needed a keen, expert eye which they both had from long years of experience. Step by slow step forward, cautiously. The almost invisible movement in the sand, and you bent down quickly to scoop the razorfish up and into the bucket.

They were now at an age where success blessed them each time they stretched down. They put the contents of their two half-filled buckets into the one and walked round the corner towards the scallop beds. Here too they knew their business, and were soon walking back to the boat with a bucketful of scallops and a bucketful of razorfish.

They cooked them in butter that night, and the world never tasted better. The spring equinox came, bringing with it the great winds and high tides which made any sailing impossible for days. May brought in beautiful calm weather which made them venture further out to the shallow banks west of the Stac where the mackerel were already plentiful, and when full summer came they could be seen daily out beyond Isle Griomail raising the pretty little green and yellow canvas sail which you could see from miles around, bringing in saithe, and hake and herring too.

It was the last and only summer. Donald failed to return from Woodstock. He wrote home saying he'd met this girl and was staying on for some time with her. They were going to travel through America and eventually make their way to the south, perhaps down as far as Patagonia and the Falklands, or even further south, and then maybe east on to Polynesia and the Fijis and on to the Far East itself.

'When something was lost,' Alasdair said, 'They would send for the *cnàimh-luirg*, the tracking-bone. Tormod Mòr Mac Iain Lèith had the gift, but he's long dead now. He would hold the sheepbone firm between his palms and follow its shake all the way to the corpse. Or to anything else you needed to find. But no one else can do it now that he's gone.'

I wasn't sure why the seeming idyll came to an end, but it did. I made some vague inquiries when I heard, but no one really seemed sure. Ill-health, some suggested, though there was no evidence for that since both Alasdair and Katell then lived on for a good number of years once they returned to the mainland. Though I know now that your loved ones' health frames your life.

The most likely explanation at the time was that they were missing their children and grandchildren, or that they were missing them. Anyway by the time All Saint's Day came round once more they'd brought the skiff back ashore again, where she was tied up and made secure for wintering within the stone byre.

That year, right enough, Hallowmas fell on a Wednesday which was always an inauspicious sign. The proverb put it this way – '*Nuair as Di-Ciadain an t-Samhain, is iarganaich na dhèidh*' –

'When Hallowmas is on a Wednesday, affliction follows.'

The boat remained there, untouched, for no one of course had the right to touch it. It didn't belong to them. It was secure anyway within the byre, and occasionally one of the villagers would peer through the small chinks in the stone to make sure she was still there, wind and watertight. She was.

In time the surprise and disappointment diminished, and even the folk who had the shared the glory day of the launch began to forget her existence, hidden away in the old steading. One day, they said, one of the children, or grandchildren, or maybe even the great-great-grandchildren will come for it, and take it out and spruce it up and relaunch it out into the great ocean. Donald might come. Or Andrew. Or Elizabeth or one of the other girls.

But they all had their reasons. Donald got no further south than Philadelphia when Susan's pregnancy forced them to stay where they were and forget, in the meantime at least, about Patagonia and the Falklands and Polynesia and the Far East. They managed to get a couple of rooms on the east side of the docklands where Donald got a job as a warehouseman, and when one pregnancy led to another they just stayed on there, largely kept by the monthly money sent to them by Susan's parents, who were business folk in New York.

Andrew returned, but had no interest in the sea and settled down in Glasgow, while Elizabeth and all the other girls rarely ventured home either once they started working and married and settled down. The old boat was their parents' dream, not theirs.

Someone – I think now that it was my late mother – told me over the phone that Alasdair and Katell had moved back to the mainland, to Aberdeen she thought, though she wasn't quite sure as they hadn't really told anyone, and hadn't left a forwarding address. I didn't really believe her at first, but she insisted.

'One of their daughters lives out that way,' she said, 'and I think they've gone to stay with her.'

I suppose any of us could have made specific enquiries, which weren't quite so easy of course in those pre-internet days, but then again we didn't want to seem inquisitive or to be interfering, when they'd evidently made a private decision which didn't really concern us. Even though it did, diminishing our lives, further fracturing our already fragile community. Though who was I to comment, being in London in the sweet arms of Margherita by that time.

In fact, they hadn't moved to Aberdeen at all, but to Aberdeenshire, which is a completely different thing. Aberdeen, after all, is a sea city, in which I could imagine them finding some solace in the grey sight of the North Sea, but in actual fact they'd moved inland to be with their daughter in the Strathdon valley, which lies about fifty miles west of the city.

It is of course a beautiful area in its own right, in the foothills of the Cairngorm Mountains, filled with deer and pheasants and grouse and all kinds of wildlife and with the famous River Don running through, and Royal Balmoral with all its history and trappings nearby, but still it was no place for a boat. I still grieve for Alasdair and Katell bound there by land and mountains, and surely – surely – pining for *The Blue Dolphin*, rotting away in the old Uist byre. O, what's the point in speaking about what they could have done? Wouldn't we all alter the universe if we could?

But they had their compensations, and we were in fact looking at some of the old photographs of Alasdair and Kate with their grandchildren just the other day when we stopped by to see them, completely unexpectedly. We'd spent the night in Aberdeen – the city, that is – ourselves, and decided to drive westwards out through Banchory and on to Balmoral before heading south.

I knew they'd lived in Corgarff, though I had no actual address, but we stopped at the local Post Office and – for once – found it was still run by someone local who remembered exactly who we were talking about.

'My mother used to be friendly with them,' she said. 'In

fact two of their grandchildren still live here. One – Katie – is married up at the old farm, and a grandson – I think he's called Alasdair – lives at the old schoolhouse which you'll have passed on the way into the village. I'm sure both of them will make you feel very welcome.'

And they did. Alasdair was a tall thin man in his early forties. He was busy mowing the lawn on one of these large petrol-driven machines when we arrived, and he had no hesitation in inviting us in. He immediately phoned his sister, but was told that she was away for a few days visiting her own daughter who was at university in St Andrews. We explained who we were of course, and he was delighted to meet up with someone who knew the 'old folk' as he called them.

'I was so young then,' he explained. 'What would I have been now? Four? Five? Six? That kind of age. But I remember them clearly. They were wonderful people. Quiet and gentle but full of stories. I wish I could remember some of them, but of course I was too young to really pay much attention to them at the time.'

And he went down into the kitchen and returned with an album. And there they were: Alasdair sitting on a garden bench with two young children on his knees.

'That's me on the left there,' said Alasdair. 'And Katie on the other knee. It's a real pity she's away, for she'd remember more.'

Then one of Katell with a golf club in her hand. Alasdair laughed.

'I think Mum and Dad tried to teach them to play golf, but they had no idea.'

The rest now blur into one – old Alasdair and Kate outside Balmoral Castle; one of them with their own daughter and son-in-law and young Alasdair and Katie at a beach somewhere.

'I think that's Stonehaven,' young Alasdair suggested – and one of the two of them standing side by side in front of a waterfall. 'That's the famous Slok of Dess on the Dee,' he said. 'I think they were really impressed by the force of water on the fall.'

He was very kind and hospitable to us, insisting that we have coffee and some of his own home made scones, which were delicious. They were straight out of the Aga. He worked as a Social Worker in the district and talked to us for a while openly and honestly about some of the issues he had to deal with, especially amongst young people.

'My own mum had a breakdown,' he explained. 'That's what brought Granny and Grampa here in the first place – to help out. It was meant to be for a while, but you know how things develop... she never really got that much better. I was just newly born when they came. I think I was maybe around nine when they passed away.'

We visited the churchyard on the way out of the village. Young Alasdair had said we couldn't miss it. 'It's the old church on the left just before the bend after the garage.'

A slight drizzle began to fall. The graves were on a mound overlooking the strath, with the names faded and difficult to make out through the tears.

I looked in every direction to see if I could catch sight of the sea, which must be somewhere, but all was land to the far horizons. I had to look up to glimpse water: and there the clouds swept eastwards, gathering pace as they headed out towards the grey North Sea.

8

THE SIXTY-YEAR-OLD woman on the train attracted little attention from anyone. Why should she? Once upon a time, a woman of her age would have been considered old, but modernity had made time obsolete. Not through Botox and surgery, but by dress and fashion. How ancient her gran had looked in those clothes, though she would have been no more than fifty at the time.

As she sat there, Helen remembered how eternally young her own mother had always looked, merely through the elixir of her enthusiasm and spirit. She had basically been too busy to grow old, and became an older version of herself, filled with endless hope and energy even well into her eighties. Even then it was all about planting: the larch and birch wood she planted on her eightieth birthday was in great shape now.

They were passing the Loch Sloy station where her father had worked. Crianlarich ahead, where the train would split into two, half heading north, the other half heading west. They stopped there for about ten minutes, while the staff uncoupled the carriages. She wanted fresh air so walked around on the platform along with the other passengers.

A group of students, waiting for the southbound train which the guard had announced would be half-an-hour late, were sitting around on the other platform. One of them, a young fair-haired man, unstrapped his guitar and began playing a tune. She recognised it instantly: 'The Foggy Dew'.

She noticed that the girl who was with him had a fiddle case. Could it? She walked over and looked down at the case. Old. Leather. Brown. With that distinctive Italian cross-stitching on the external trim.

'Excuse me,' she said. 'Do you think you could join in with your friend and play a tune? I used to play the fiddle myself when I was younger, and I would so love to hear a good tune again. Out here in the open air.'

The girl smiled.

'Sure,' she said. 'No problem.'

She unzipped the case and there inside was a somewhat battered old fiddle which wasn't the lost violin. The girl raised the fiddle to her shoulder, tuned it for a few moments, and joined in her boyfriend's tune which was now a slow air which Helen did not recognise. Her train was leaving in three minutes. But it was her fiddle case. Of that she was certain.

'How – I mean where did you get the case?' she asked.

The girl took it as an innocent question: someone admiring the old leather.

'O. From a neighbour. An old man who has lots of what he calls junk about the house. He was getting rid of it all and asked all his neighbours to take whatever they needed and give something to charity in return. But his junkyard is still as full as ever! I got the fiddle there too. It's not much good, is it?'

She jumped on to the train, while the guard raised his whistle at the end of the platform. 'Have you a card?' she asked the girl. 'Sometimes I hold ceilidhs,' she lied 'and maybe the two of you could play at it.'

The girl handed her a card through the window as Helen's train began to move.

'Julie Stone,' the card read. 'Trinity Road, Edinburgh,' with a website and mobile number.

The train climbed through the hazel trees on the lower slope of Strath Fillan. She knew the route well enough: the slow ascent to Tyndrum then down through Glen Lochy to Lochaweside, the Pass of Brander and on to Taynuilt and in by Loch Etive to Oban itself. Loch Awe.

Why hadn't she thought of it before? Instead of going on to Oban for the night she could stop there and get the next day's train in for the ferry. Loch Awe where her parents had first stayed when they were first married, under the shadow of Ben Cruachan.

'*Cruachan Beann, Cruachan Beann, Cruachan Beann, 's mòr mo thlachd dhìot*': the song that old Seonaidh Dhùghaill had always sung at the Dervaig cèilidhs!

She checked. She had a signal. A quick few movements and she accessed the hotel's home page. Yes, they had a room for the night: one with a view of the loch, and out towards Ben Cruachan itself. They had a car which could pick her up, free of charge. Which meant, of course, that it was built into the room's price – but that was fine. Loch Awe here needed business as much as LA there.

The room was beautiful. The building had originally been built as a shooting lodge for Campbell of Brander but was now owned by a retired MP and her husband, who had renewed and upgraded it into a luxury retreat. They had retained many of the gorgeous old features of the building, including the twin stone lions which adorned the entrance, with a plume of water spouting from their open mouths.

'Victoriana at its worst,' said Lady Creggan, who personally signed her in.

'At its best, I think,' said Helen.

She gazed out over the well kept lawns and the rose gardens which were in full bloom far below. Loch Awe itself was quiet, without any movement. Ben Cruachan still retained banks of snow on its northernmost tops.

Was it really possible? Of course it was: much stranger things had happened. She would have recognised that case anywhere: it was impossible that another, of that vintage, with that cross-stitching right there, and that tiny dent next the handle still there, could exist. She laughed. As if it really mattered! Which of course it did: the loss had circled her life.

Maybe that was sufficient, however. Be satisfied with that glimpse, that knowledge, that moment. For where else could it lead, except either to disappointment or satisfaction when she finally traced that old loss down to – what? – a cellar, or a junk room in an old man's house in Edinburgh? Better to live in anticipation, and all that...

She decided to go for a walk. She would have her bath later. She opened the windows wide and felt the chill, so she put on her thick coat and went outside down into the gardens. The roses were even more beautiful from close up: real authentic old ones which hadn't been spoilt by the removal of the thorns, so that not only did they look lovely, but also smelt like roses. She recognised many of them – the orange Alexanders with their sweet scent, the salmon pink New Zealands, the bright red Royal Williams with their heady smell, and the wonderfully named Jude the Obscure, with its yellow chalice-shaped blooms.

She was the most unlikely convert. And it had happened so simply too. No great big revelation or angels singing from the heavens, but a quiet Sabbath evening in Chichester Cathedral where she'd gone to listen to the music. Handel's Messiah was scheduled for 8pm, but she arrived early – around four – and wandered round the building. The light was astonishing, and at its most luminous through Marc Chagall's window.

She hadn't really realised that a service was about to begin, but when she heard the opening choral hymn felt that she couldn't walk out. So she sat there quietly in a side pew. How wonderful the choir sounded, in their long red and white robes. Sancte Deus, Sancte Fortis, Sancte Immortalis, with the sweet young voices rising into the heavens.

It happened to be a visiting preacher – the Rev Dr John Stott – who talked about Mary going to Jesus at the wedding in Cana and saying to him 'They have run out of wine.' And Dr Stott simply said one little thing which caused Helen to 'give her heart to Jesus' as the evangelicals put it. 'She only told Him what He already knew – but that turned plain water into rich wine.'

He expanded and expounded, of course, about omnipotence and omniscience, but it was the simple transformation, as it were, that struck her. His mother told him a fact and that truth had triggered the miracle. She looked up towards Chagall's stained-glass window: practically speaking, small pieces of glass held together by strips of lead and supported by a rigid frame, but in reality a hymn of praise to God. That was the spark. This was not silica with adds of potash and soda and lime and oxides, but life, and life in all its fullness, as the Reverend Stott was declaring. Perhaps Klee's churches could be unboxed. Black could be white.

She went down through the wicker gate at the bottom of the rose garden, which led on to the path which took her down by the river to the loch itself. Something stirred in the water, though she couldn't make out what. Likely a salmon or trout, for the loch was famous for both, though you now needed a permit from the hotel to fish for them. Not that she would need one, for it came with the room. Though she wouldn't use that either. Then she saw what had stirred, as the otter climbed out of the water and disappeared into the reeds beds on the bank. Native American medicine implied that if an otter swam into your life the message was to rid yourself of worry and pain.

How necessary animals were. Ótr he was called in Norse mythology. Ótr the dwarf, the son of King Hreidmar and the brother of Fafnir and Regin. He could change into any form, and used to spend many days in the shape of an otter, greedily eating fish. Until he was slain accidentally by Loki. His father, Hreidmar, demanded a large weregild in return for Ótr's death – namely to fill Ótr's skin with yellow gold and then to cover it entirely with red gold. However, when the skin was covered in gold, one whisker was still protruding which ultimately caused the death of Hreidmar and his two equally avaricious sons. One small thing. Surely that wasn't the fiddle, gnawing away at her soul?

Who stole the baby? She began to hum the song quietly under her breath –

Òbhan òbhan,
Goiridh òg O,
Goiridh òg O,
Goiridh òg O,
Òbhan òbhan,
Goiridh òg O,
Cha d' fhuair mi lorg mo chaoineachain.

I left my baby lying here, lying here, lying here, I left my baby lying here, to go and gather blaeberries. I found the wee brown otter's track, otter's track, otter's track, I found the wee brown otter's track, But ne'er a trace o' my baby, O.

It must have been supernatural. No human being could be so sour as to steal a baby. It was better to blame the fairies than the fathers. Everything else was found – the otter, the swan, the duck, the red-speckled calf, the cow in the mud, the mist on the mountain – but ne'er a trace o' baby, O. Always the external cause, the criminal from outside.

She rose from the lochside and walked back in to the hotel through the rose garden. She ate alone at the small round table next to the bay window. The food too was exquisite: local lamb with fresh vegetables from the hotel's own garden, followed by fruits from the orchard. She drank mint tea, and went upstairs. In the bath, she resumed reading the book: Alain-Fournier's *Le Grand Meaulnes*. Having read it several times in translation, she was finally getting round to reading slowly through it in the original French.

C'est le dimanche seulement, dans l'après-midi, que je
résolus de sonner à la porte des Sablonnières. Tandis
que je grimpais les coteaux dénudés, j'entendais sonner
au loin les vêpres du dimanche d'hiver. Je me sentais
solitaire et désolé. Je ne sais quel pressentiment triste

m'envahissait. Et je ne fus qu'à demi surpris lorsque, à mon coup de sonnette, je vis M. de Galais tout seul paraître et me parler à voix basse: Yvonne de Galais était alitée, avec une fièvre violente; Meaulnes avait dû partir dès vendredi matin pour un long voyage; on ne sait quand il reviendrait...

The words made less sense than the meaning.

'I must still be filtering it through the English versions I've read,' she said out loud. 'Like everything.'

She put the book down and lay back deep in the bath, covering herself with water to the tip of her nose. Helen. Helen O' Connor. And how, as soon as people heard her name, they instantly assumed she was Irish. Which she sort of was: half was by genetics, and as for the rest... Helen, the Gaelic *Eilidh*, the French *Hélène*, the Greek *Eleni*. Ah! The great original. *Eilidh na Tròidhe*. Helen of Troy. And the other great Helen, of Kirkconnel.

She was out of the bath and switched on her iPod, for the great Burns version of the song:

O that I were where Helen lies
Night and day on me she cries;
O that I were where Helen lies
In fair Kirkconnel lee.

She sang with it, pretending too that she had a fiddle:

O Helen fair beyond compare
A ringlet of thy flowing hair
I'll wear it still for ever mair
Until the day I die.

She let the bathrobe slip off and surrendered herself to the song, her left hand rapidly playing the chords, her right hand bowing the strings –

Curs'd be the hand that shot the shot
And curs'd the gun that gave the crack!
Into my arms bird Helen lap
And died for sake o' me!
O think na ye but my heart was sair
My love fell down and spake nae mair
There did she swoon we meikle care
On fair Kirkconnel lee...

She lay back on the bed, quiet, reducing the iPod level with the remote to a whisper. All was still except for the voice coming from the machine: I wish I were where Helen lies, Night and day on me she cries, And I am weary of the skies, For her sake that died for me. She would take up her paintbrush again. She slept. Birds were singing. Willow warblers, mistle thrushes and a solitary stonechat: she would recognise its call anywhere. It was a beautiful sunny morning. The iPod must have been playing softly all night: she turned Helen off.

She caught the 9.30 train into Oban, which connected with the ongoing ferry to Mull. It was packed with summer visitors, most of whom – by their conversations – were heading for Iona. She managed to get a bench seat for herself outside on the top deck and watched the familiar landsights fade behind them: the red granite of St Columba's Cathedral, the folly that was McCaig's, the ruin of Dunstaffnage, the flashing lighthouse at Ganavan, the flat green point of Kerrera. They sailed through the channel where the Firth of Lorne met the Lynn of Lorne, and were soon rounding Duart Point with Craignure ahead and the Sound of Mull itself stretching on towards the past.

I had no idea it was her. It was sheer chance that I happened to be on that particular ferry, for I had originally intended to travel a week earlier, but had been delayed by some stupid visa issues connected with Marion's ashes. I'd promised to take them up and scatter them on her native Yorkshire Moors. She'd been quite specific about the location – Rosedale on the north-eastern side of the River Severn, where she'd spent many happy days as a young girl.

The mistake I made was telling the British authorities that I was taking her ashes with me: the French didn't care, but as soon as I arrived at the airport and declared the casket to the airline, they insisted on phoning immigration and this debate ensued about whether ashes were or were not covered by the trans-European right to travel. Of course they were and I knew that, and they knew that, and we all knew that, but procedures are procedures and it took a week to get official clearance. I was lucky, of course: it could have taken forever.

I got smart after that, and as soon as I rebooked my flight for London I just put dear Marion's ashes into a tobacco pouch and travelled with her in my jacket pocket. We were frisked at security of course, but they let us through once I assured them that she wasn't a drug. I caught the train from London to York and then hired a small car so that I could drive out into the solitude of the moors to pay the last respects. It rained all day and for a while I took sanctuary in Rosedale Abbey, and by the time I came out the rain had ceased and rainbows adorned the countryside on all sides.

I parked the car at the upper end of the Severn and walked up through the dale in the early evening. It was lovely, gentle countryside. A landscape I was more or less unfamiliar with, and so different from both the Scottish countryside and the French terrain with which I had become acquainted. It was good farming land: that was evident from the amount of lush grass on the lower slopes. It got barer, of course, as I climbed, but the crofters I'd known in my childhood would still have envied the riches of these exposed uplands.

I paused for a good while at the peak, looking all around and sharing that last spectacular view with Marion: the splendour of the Cleveland Hills to our north and west, all the dales running away down at our feet – Bransdale and Farndale and Newtondale and Rosedale itself – and away to the east the North Sea beyond the far lights of Whitby and Scarborough which we could now see sparkling up in the twilight.

We waited until that moment arrived when it was neither quite day nor night: when there was sufficient light still to distinguish earth from sky and land from sea, but not enough to locate anywhere, to differentiate town from city or cattle from people. And at that moment, as the dots on the horizon became all indistinguishable, I let her go, up out of my hands into the air where all was invisible because no stars shone, and no moon had yet emerged.

They emerged as I descended. The moon itself was a full moon, shining with a sudden liquid brightness all over the moors. Things which had been indistinct in the ascent became eerily illuminated in the descent: here was a hidden waterfall, and over there, where I thought I'd seen a stone wall, were the ruins of an old Roman fort. Stars appeared, dwarfing the twinkling earth lights that were spread all around, and I confess I allowed myself to believe that the sparkling one which shone so brightly a bit to the left of the moon was Marion, now liberated from all her pain and cares.

I slept in the car that night as I had forgotten to book anywhere. I had done no forward planning, but the visit back home to Scotland must have been in the back of my mind as I'd prepared to scatter the ashes, for next morning I turned on the car's sat nav and typed in Scotland and followed the disembodied woman's voice who steered me all the way through Grosmont and Guisborough and all the other now forgotten places which brought me back up to the border.

I breakfasted somewhere near Hexham I think, and by lunchtime had crossed the Cheviots and was in Jedburgh, where I stopped for the rest of the day. I booked into a little hotel near the town square and slept all afternoon, dreaming that I was back home.

When I woke of course I realised I was: the stuff in the hotel room made it unmistakable. Bonny Scotland pictures all over the place, which I'd been too tired to really notice earlier when I checked in. I had a shower and went down to the bar which was adorned with a marble bust of Sir Walter.

Beside the bar was a scroll on which was written, in rounded calligraphy, his most famous couplet, 'Oh what a tangled web we weave, When first we practice to deceive'. On the other side of the lounge was a matching scroll declaring, 'Breathes there the man with soul so dead, Who never to himself hath said, This is my own, my native land'. The television was on in the corner, showing some pictures of Rupert Murdoch.

The Borders are as good a place as any to decide the future. I really had no notion what to do in the coming days. I had no pressing reason to go back to Paris – in truth, no pressing reason to go anywhere, even though I knew that I wanted to settle things up in Paris and leave. Too many dying memories.

And it had been such a long time since I'd been to Scotland. Been home, if that was the word. For what had this southern place to do with me? Nothing much, going by this unfair analysis from the Borders hotel, with its romantic call still on the walls while a different global empire ruled the waves. Ach! Scoatland sma'? Nothing bu' heather! How marvellously descriptive. And incomplete. This girning land. I should head tae Dundee! Pa Broon Land, whaur I micht see Oor Wullie. Jings crivvens help ma boab!

So I phoned the car hire company in the morning and told them I'd like to extend the car hire for a month as I planned to spend some time travelling round Scotland. I drove north through the lovely forests of Lauderdale and arrived in Edinburgh from the south, via Dalkieth. I took the bypass round Edinburgh itself, past Swanston, spurning its attractions, and marvelled afresh at the great beauty of the Forth Rail Bridge to my right, then took the coast road round Fife, through the pretty little seafront villages of St Monans, Pittenweem and Anstruther and Crail so that I could lunch at St Andrews.

'Here for the golf?' asked the barman who served lunch.

'No. Just travelling. Northwards.'

'Far?'

'Dundee anyway,' I responded.

He laughed. 'It's a braw city. Gone all fancy too. Do you know they're building a new V&A there?'

It didn't mean anything to me.

'Victoria and Albert. Art Galley. Dundee's become the new art capital of the world.'

'Wasn't it always the art centre of the world? The *Beano* and *Dandy* and all that...?'

'Good old DC Thomson,' he said. 'What did they use to say – Jute, Jam and Journalism? Not much of that about nowadays, eh?'

Some real golfers had entered, so he went off to serve them.

Who can tell – maybe he changed my life? Had he not summed it up so well I might have been tempted to go on up to Dundee, but I decided to leave it, and go west instead. Too many professors everywhere. Back in the car I checked the map from the glove compartment: there were so many options. Could I find a blacksmith anywhere, or a forge?

I decided on the A91 to Perth then the A85 west through Crieff and Lochearnhead. I filled the tank up again and clicked the information into the sat nav and headed for Cupar. I'd forgotten. There it was: Luvians Ice cream shop. Run by the Fusaros. One of their boys, Tony, had been at university with me, and it was now almost fifty years since I'd seen him. I stopped the car and went in and asked if he was about.

'No,' said the young woman behind the counter. 'Uncle Tony deals with the wine importing side of the business. He's in Spain just now on business.'

The ice cream was lovely. Home made with the best of products, and just the right consistency and sweetness. Summer's honey breath. Afterwards, I regretted that I hadn't bought one of Tony's fine wine's for Helen, but the opportunity was lost.

I spent the night in a B&B at Lochearnhead and left very early in the morning so that I could catch the first ferry. I planned to go on to Uist later on in the week but thought first

I would spend a day or two around the Oban area.

Maybe it was Marion's death and the holiness of the departure on the Yorkshire Dales, but I had a notion to visit Iona, of all places. Strangely, I'd never been there, despite its reasonable proximity to some of my childhood haunts. I think it's reputation for 'spirituality' had made me pretty cautious about it, and every time I'd thought about visiting, the whole idea of bus-loads of New Age tourists descending on the island had put me off.

And here I was now, one of these very people! Even though I kidded myself that I was different – more or less a local, and not one to be fooled or swayed by spiritual chanting and fragrant candles on an isolated island.

Which, of course, is how I found myself that morning on the very same ferry as Helen, after all these years. Coincidence is a strange thing, for the two of us then researched it, from the Mathematical Coincidences of Dimension to the Computer Simulation of Alignment, ranging from the Jung-Pauli Theory of Synchronicity to Kammerer's Theory of Seriality, though we preferred Einstein's famous definition that 'coincidence is God's way of remaining anonymous'.

And no wonder He wants to remain anonymous, if the Internet is anything to go by. The whole thing is mad, for chance is nothing, and one night we Googled the word to find this marvel flashing up before our eyes –

Bizarre! Some Amazing Coincidences!

CHILDHOOD BOOK: While American novelist Anne Parrish was browsing bookstores in Paris in the 1920s, she came upon a book that was one of her childhood favourites – *Jack Frost and Other Stories*. She picked up the old book and showed it to her husband, telling him of the book she fondly remembered as a child. Her husband took the book, opened it, and on the flyleaf found the inscription 'Anne Parrish, 209 N. Weber Street, Colorado

Springs.' It was Anne's very own book.

ROYAL COINCIDENCE: In Monza, Italy, King Umberto I
went to a small restaurant for dinner, accompanied by
his aide-de-camp, General Emilio Ponzia-Vaglia. When
the owner took King Umberto's order, the King noticed
that he and the restaurant owner were virtual doubles, in
face and in build. Both men began discussing the striking
resemblances between each other and found many more
similarities –

1. Both men were born on the same day, of the
same year (14th March, 1844).
2. Both men had been born in the same town.
3. Both men married a woman with the same
name, Margherita.
4. The restaurateur opened his restaurant on the
same day that King Umberto was crowned King
of Italy.
5. On the 29th July 1900 King Umberto was
informed that the restaurateur had died that
day in a mysterious shooting accident, and as he
expressed his regret, he was then assassinated by
an anarchist in the crowd.

GOLDEN SCARAB: From *The Structure and Dynamics
of the Psyche* by Carl Jung – 'A young woman I was
treating had, at a critical moment, a dream in which she
was given a golden scarab. While she was telling me this
dream I sat with my back to the closed window. Suddenly
I heard a noise behind me, like a gentle tapping. I turned
round and saw a flying insect knocking against the
window pane from outside. I opened the window and
caught the creature in the air as it flew in. It was the
nearest analogy to the golden scarab that one finds in our
latitudes, a scarabaeid beetle, the common rose chafer
(*Cetonia aurata*) which contrary to its usual habits had

felt an urge to get into a dark room at this particular moment. I must admit that nothing like it ever happened to me before or since, and that the dream of the patient has remained unique in my experience'.

We held hands and laughed and were astonished in equal measures.

'Look,' said Helen, 'that's nothing compared to the comments!'

And they were pretty astonishing: Chad HXC commented,

'Hey, these are pretty crazy, but here is one not mentioned. Jesus's birthday was September 11, 3BC. The attack on the twin towers was on September 11, 2001. Which is also the number for the emergency crew 9-1-1.'

The Dum Guy responded,

'Chad HXC – Are you joking? I wasn't aware that Christ's birthday was known to the day and month, although I've heard Jesus was a Leo.'

And topped off by Drogo, who wrote later on the thread –

'We went to Disney World, a trip almost 2000 miles from home. In a shop on Main Street we came across our neighbours from down the street.'

'The world's mad,' I said.

'Well, no madder than us,' was her response.

9

IT JUST HAPPENED that this time it was the opposite way round: she was descending the stairs, and I was climbing.

'Sorry,' she said, trying to stand to one side, and I must have smiled and said, 'O, don't worry – I'll get by.'

I might have said that – I've really no idea. Anyway the meeting on the stairs reminded me of something, from a long time ago, and it was only afterwards as I sat on the deck upstairs that all things became possible.

No, it couldn't be, I said to myself. The stairs are narrow and you're bound to meet hundreds of folk on them if you go up and down, and what else would you say anyway in that awkward situation except for 'Sorry,' and 'O, don't worry – I'll get by.'

And of course I'd felt no urge to touch the old lady's arm as she passed. Not at my age anyway.

Downstairs, Helen hadn't given it a second thought. She was in the boat's small bookshop, which was selling all the usual tourist junk – plastic crocodiles, Loch Ness Monsters, Isle of Mull keyrings, Columban medallions. Even the book-stall was small and limited – mostly picture books of old ferries and puffers and steamers. What a great business nostalgia was. She bought a magazine – The Scottish Field – to while away some time.

We both disembarked at Craignure. Long gone were the days

when this great ferry service would then sail on to Tobermory and Colonsay and Tiree and Castlebay and Lochboisdale. Now everyone had their own ferry. This was really like a large shuttle bus now, transporting mostly tourists backwards and forwards between Mull and the mainland every three-quarters of an hour. At least in the summer.

The days of the bicycle too were gone: Helen was going to catch the service bus north where she would pick up her own old car which she used whenever she returned to the island. I'd left my hire car parked safely at the pier in Oban, and was going to join the tour bus which took all the visitors on down to Fionnphort from where we would all get the smaller ferry across to Iona.

None of it happened. As we were queuing to disembark, I bumped into her again in the crowd at the top of the gangway. I nodded to her, for having spoken to her earlier on the stairway, we almost seemed like acquaintances. She had a rucksack, and since I was just over for the day, I only carried a small shoulderbag. I acted the gentleman.

'Would you like a hand?' I asked.

She hesitated.

'Yeah. Sure – just down to the bottom of these stairs.'

I gave her my hand luggage and swung her rucksack on my shoulder.

'Thanks,' she said, at the bottom.

'Can I carry it to your car?' I asked.

'No,' she said. 'No thanks. My car's not here. I'm just getting that service bus.'

'Is that the one to Fionnphort?' I asked.

'No,' she said. 'The one for Fionnphort is over there. This is the one for the north end of the island, going to Tobermory then on to Dervaig and Calgary and down the west coast.'

She looked at me, and pointed to the buses.

'It says all that on the bus. See? Tobermory on that one. Fionnphort on the other.'

I looked for signs of sarcasm, but could not detect any.

Maybe she thought I was plain stupid. Or couldn't read English. Sometimes, to be fair, I'd adopt a French accent and having recently lived there, that was perfectly plausible. Or maybe she just thought I was at it: a real fly-by-night, a real chancer, who went around trying to pick up women. How life had made us suspicious.

'Great,' I said. 'That's the bus I was going to get. North, and round the west coast.'

'Are you sure?' she replied. 'Normally folk come here just to go on to Iona.'

'Yes. Yes, I'm sure.'

I sat halfway along the bus and was relieved that she sat opposite me when she entered, even though there were plenty empty seats further away. We smiled, and of course I knew then it was her: the freckles were still there, and the smile, and the eyes, even if the dark curly hair was now short and rooted grey.

'So,' she said. 'Imagine that! Would you call it a – miracle? Or a coincidence?'

I was overwhelmed – not by the miracle, or the coincidence, but by her confession of remembrance.

'But you had no reason…' I began.

'No, of course not,' she said. 'Except that I was in trauma that day and maybe because of that I remember it all.'

'Trauma?'

She looked at me across the bus divide.

'Yes. I'd lost my violin, and I think I was in shock. It made me hugely sensitive to everything around me, as if I could suddenly hear or see or find my fiddle in the most unexpected of places, and I must therefore have been highly tuned to every single thing, in case – somehow and magically and miraculously – my violin would manifest itself somewhere. It didn't, but everything else did. I remember the exact colour and shape and texture of the bench at Waverley where I lost my fiddle. I remember the voices of all the police officers and of all the pawn shop owners I asked. I remember the sound of the train going through all the stations up here as

I travelled to tell my Mum. I remember this man who blocked my way on the stairs and how he said "Sorry" as he tried to stand to one side, and how I said, "O, don't worry – I'll get by," and I remember how I cycled all the way home – I can still hear the sound of the wheels on the road and the willow warblers singing, and I can smell the wild garlic – and how my Mum was milking Daisy down by the gate, and how she sensed I was there, and turned, still sitting on her stool and waved to me.'

It was a glorious flood of words and I was terribly ashamed of my earlier lies and my manoeuvring to get to know her, when it was obvious she knew all along.

'I'm sorry,' I began, but she stopped me with a wave of her hand.

'No. Don't say it,' she said. 'Be honest.'

She moved across in her seat to be nearer the aisle and looked straight at me.

'For a change?' she asked.

I lowered my eyes, even looked the other way for a moment, out the window.

'We're not children any more. It doesn't work like that any more.'

I looked back at her, trying to smile. I wished too I had the courage to move nearer, even towards the aisle, but even that was lacking. Maybe truth had frozen me.

'So,' I said instead, maybe foolishly, 'Did you ever find the violin?'

She shook her head, slowly. I moved nearer the aisle.

'Listen – I know this sounds all foolish and daft and sort of made-up and as if I'm saying it because you're here and I want to bed you and all that stuff we know and read about, but still it's true.'

I paused. I managed to pause.

'But I've – I've wondered about you all my life. Who you were, what you were, how you were, where you were, what happened to you, what didn't happen to you, did you marry, did you have children, did you live, did you die, did it matter, did I make it up, did any of it happen, ever...'

She leaned over towards me and did the most beautiful thing: stroked my cheek, as if I were a little child.

'You've wondered about yourself,' she said.

Or at least that's what I think she said.

'Who you were, what you were, how you were, where you were, what happened to you, what didn't happen to you, did you marry, did you have children, did you live, did you die, did it matter, did you make it up, did any of it happen, ever...'

She paused, fully withdrawing her hand.

'And I only know all that because that's what we've all wondered. You don't need to be a prophet to see it. Though you might need to be one to hear it.'

Afterwards, as we walked down the road towards Dervaig, things were discovered: a disused apiary by the roadside, a finch's nest in a bush by the river, and a discarded, though not quite broken, child's bicycle in the ditch.

Once we arrived at Tobermory, the joining bus west wasn't there – it had broken down – so we just decided to walk to Helen's home in Calgary instead.

'It's sixteen miles,' she said, looking me up and down like a horse. 'Do you think you'll manage?'

'No,' I said. 'I don't think I'll manage. But I've got a good thumb, and if needs be...'

She shook her head.

'I don't think so. Two reasons – first of all, there's not much traffic on this road. And secondly – don't you think hitching is a bit – what shall I say – uncool? – for folks of our age?'

So we tramped it, like two young road trippers. It was a beautiful day anyway – a May day, with sufficient sun to be warm and enough wind to be cool. In the proper sense. I sensed she'd lied about the first part, for there seemed to me to be more than enough cars on the road, and occasionally one would stop and offer us a lift, but we refused, saying that we were out enjoying the day. Which we were.

She told me about Peru and Madagascar and the Rhonda

Valley and I told her some of the things about Alasdair and Kate, and Big Roderick, and the boat, and London. But though we told these things, yet we told them as relative strangers, for it is one thing to hear a story and another to trust it.

We finally accepted a lift from a local. We knew he was local because we could hear his exhaust from miles away. He stopped his old Cortina and beckoned us in. He came out of the car and flung the rucksack and my hand luggage into the boot, steered Helen into the front passenger seat and off we headed.

We were all silent for a while, mostly because we could hardly think, never mind speak or hear, because of the racket from the exhaust. But after some miles we became accustomed to it and spoke our words between the bullet sounds. He started.

'Aye aye.'

'Aye,' we replied.

'Aye,' he said in return.

'Well Helen O' Connor,' he then said, 'it's really splendid to see you again.'

He looked over at her.

'And you looking so well too. As beautiful today as you were when I first set eyes upon you, but no wonder, for your mother too was a beautiful woman.'

'Now, now, Lachlan,' said Helen. 'You know it's not fair to compare a daughter with her mother.'

He laughed. And looked in the car mirror.

'And who's this splendid gentleman who has the honour of walking the roads with you?'

I'd known instantly from his accent that he was a Gaelic speaker, so I said.

'*Uibhisteach. Tuigidh tu fhèin an còrr.*'

He laughed raucously.

'*An Uibhisteach*! They're almost as rare here as Muileachs themselves!'

He turned once again to Helen.

'Great people, the Uibhisteachs – the best sailors in the world. But that's the last thing you want to hear – my yarns about sailing the high seas with the Uist boys. And the Lewis lads – they weren't bad either!'

We all went quiet again.

'You'll want to – to go out in the boat, of course?' he said to Helen.

She nodded.

'Tomorrow?' he asked. 'Or the day after?'

'Tomorrow,' Helen said. 'You know I always like to do that first.'

He dropped us off at her house.

'You know, of course...' I began.

She waited for me to continue.

'I'll just walk on. Or there must be a B&B around here I can stay at.'

'Yes,' she said. 'There are several B&Bs around here. And there's also a taxi – Murdo the Taxi – who could take you back for the last ferry if you're that keen.'

She looked at me.

'There's also a spare room. You could sleep there.'

She raised her rucksack on her shoulders. She put it down again.

'It's not a deal. It's just pure simple humanity. With all its hopes and dangers.'

The house was cold, but we soon got a fire going and by the time we'd made tea and some food the house was warm enough. Ah! I suddenly thought. I've got nothing extra with me. 'Ehm... I was supposed to be just going to Iona for the day.'

She looked at me.

'That's what comes from telling lies! Weren't you ever in the Boy Scouts? Be prepared, and all that...'

'No,' I confessed. 'No. I'm afraid I was never in the Boy Scouts. A deprived childhood and all that...'

'Just as well I was in the Guides then.'

She went through to the back room and came back with a toothbrush and toothpaste.

'Sorry there's no shaver,' she said. 'And if you look in that old chest there, who knows what wonderful clothes you might find for yourself.'

She put on some music while I rummaged through the sea chest. Shostakovich, Symphony No 5 in D Minor, the Russian National Orchestra, conducted by Yakov Kreizberg. I sang a different song under my breath: three fat men on a dead man's chest, yo-ho-ho and a bottle of rum, as I searched out thick woolly stockings, a long striped nightshirt which Ebenezer Balfour of Shaws himself would have been proud of, a lovely hand-woven silk shirt and a couple of old-fashioned fishermen's smocks, which were old enough to be new and retro.

I felt like a little boy. Let loose in a toy shop. And I think I played the part. I put on the smock and did a pretend sailor's hornpipe, and finally piped down only when I realised something far more important was going on around me: Kreizberg was leading us quietly into the third movement, and the elegy was overwhelming. We both sat humbled.

We sat facing each other by the fireside. The flames freckled her face in the evening light and I sipped a soft malt in a crystal glass. She had a glass of red wine. Chet Baker was singing. The logs crackled, turning red. It was the time before we began to put ourselves in the story. The time when the story was still out there, to be brought into the house, rather than born within. The pre-love time when intimacy is approached rather than achieved. The way you ascend a hill from the side or the way you tack or jib when sailing a boat into the wind.

We told tales about things that had happened to us rather than about ourselves. 'I mind that time,' she said, and I would respond 'Once...' I told her about coincidences in my own life and she told about the time she was in Dublin and sitting in Bewley's tearoom thinking about her flatmate from twenty years before, Anne, when who walked in the door but... and then I remembered walking in New York and suddenly glancing up to see my name on a street sign: Alexander Street. She laughed.

'Och that could happen anywhere. Just think of the number of Alexander Streets there are!'

And of course she's right – they're everywhere, from St Petersburg to Glasgow. 'And anyway,' she said, 'you're not really Alexander at all. But Alasdair. In the same way I'm not really Helen but Eilidh.'

Again the marvel of being two things at once. A Gaelic name and an English name. Helen on one side of the fire, I on the other. The wood burning in the fire and disappearing. Chet Baker, long dead, singing softly into our ceilidh. The two languages we half-contained, half-remembered, half-forgotten. How could I tell her that I loved her. Which, like God, cannot exist without evidence.

The little people lived underground. They caroused there, to put it simply. Danced and played music and enjoyed themselves. Lived life to the full. When you see the sandy hollows on the machair that's when you really begin to believe in them. How sheltered the dunes were, protected by wave after wave of grass even in the bitterest north wind. There you could dance. You heard the music first – faint and distant, and as you approached, if the light was good, you could see the little figures playing in the reeds. A door opened and when you entered the lights all shone and the wine vats were overflowing and a little old man with a long white beard beckoned you in to sit right by him up near the fire. A piper played and all the young women in their green and silver gowns danced on the tips of their toes before being lifted high by the young men who then swept in like a fire, raising them up towards the ceiling and whirling them about the hall. The table was laden with the best of food and drink – *sitheann* (venison) and butter and green apples and porridge kail and wine in gold goblets and milk in frothing churns – and the feast was endless, day after day, night after night. When you needed to rest one of the young maidens led you through the mirrored hall to the draped rooms where a golden light shone on you as you fell asleep and when you woke the young harpist would be sitting in the corner of your room playing the *òran maidne*, the dawn chorus.

If you were fortunate you were trapped there for a hundred years and emerged still young while the whole world had died. Some took that as a curse, grieving for what had gone, like Rip Van Winkle in that other culture mourning for what had gone, confused by what remained. Others, like my old neighbour Iain Dhòmhnaill Sheumais, eased into the new dispensation, gently reminding anyone who cared to listen that Borodino hadn't been as bad as Tolstoy had made out and that the real tragedy was the terrible loss of the MacLeans at the Battle of Inverkeithing. And when you left them they always gave you butter on an ember, porridge kail in a creel, and paper shoes, and sent you away with a big gun bullet on a road of glass till you found yourself sitting right there at home.

Helen smiled. I placed some more logs on the fire and put the kettle on. It had very little to do with coincidences and everthing to do with possibilities. Or at least with hopes and dreams. That one day poverty and toil would cease and life would be all singing and dancing. That one day the earth would open and the dead would rise and that when you went back all was changed, changed utterly. That Donald would return through the smirr, that Margherita would be standing there statuesque in the evening light, that Big Roderick would stay sober forever.

I poured the coffee. It was one of those damned pots which always leaked no matter how carefully you poured. And I suppose that's when I realised that lives, like stories, were made up out of errors and faults. Coincidences dressed up as fate, hopes and fears dressed up as fairies and fauns. For to live otherwise was to die, to allow the coffee to drip on to the floor, the logs on the stove to go cold, our love to wither.

'Did your mum do the same?' I asked.

'The same what?'

'This,' I said, sipping the poured coffee from the saucer.

'No,' said Helen. 'My mum never drank coffee. Always tea. But yes, she sometimes sipped from a saucer.'

She went over to the biscuit cupboard and brought out a packet of Digestives.

'And always – always – dipped her digestive into her tea. Like this.'

It was, likely, a turning point. Where the domestic became normal, significant.

'And what about toast?' I asked.

'Sometimes,' she said.

So I went over to the cutlery cupboard and fetched out the longtailed fork and stuck it into a piece of bread and knelt by the fire, holding the loaf towards the flames.

'Too near,' Helen said. 'Far too near. You need to take it back an inch or so.'

Which I did.

'My hand's getting burnt,' I complained.

'Cry baby,' she said.

So I altered hands, toasting first this side of the bread, then the other.

It tasted wonderful with the butter melting into the grooves.

'And what about the flames then?' she asked.

'The flames?'

'Aye. The flames. Didn't they predict the future where you came from?'

'No.'

'Well, they did here.'

'And?'

'And,' she said, going on her knees beside me in front of the fire, 'the flames predict...'

She looked into the fire and I followed her gaze. The log flames were sparkling blue. Elm wood.

'The flames predict,' she said, 'that the future is golden. The ashes that fall down are memory and the smoke that rises is reason. One has given heat, the other light.'

We sat on the floor by the fire, not touching, and told stories. I told her about the fox and the wren and the smith and the fairies and the Barra widow's son and she told me that once upon a time there was a hen that had flown up and perched on an oak tree for the night and when night came she dreamed that unless she got to Dovrefjell the world would come to an end. So that very minute she jumped down and set out on her way and when she had walked a little bit she met a cockerel. 'Good day, Cocky-Locky,' said the hen.

'Good day, Henny-Penny,' said the cockerel. 'Where are you going this early in the morning?'

'Oh, I'm going to the Dovrefjell that the world might not come to an end,' said the hen, and 'Who told you that?' asked the cockerel.

'Oh, I sat in the oak and dreamt it last night,' said the hen, so 'I'll go with you,' said the cockerel.

And of course they walked on for a bit and then they met a duck, Ducky-Lucky, and a goose, Goosey-Poosey, and fox, Foxey-Cocksy who was too smart to be taken in by this dream.

'Stuff and nonsense,' said the Fox. 'The world won't come to an end if you don't get there. No! Come home with me instead to my earth, which is far better, for it's warm and jolly there.'

And, well, Henny-Penny and Cocky-Locky and Ducky-Lucky and Goosey-Poosey went off with Foxy-Cocksy to his earth and when they went in the fox laid on lots of fuel so that they all got very sleepy. The duck and the goose settled themselves into a corner but the cockerel and the hen flew up on a post. So when the goose and the duck were well asleep the fox took the goose and laid him on the embers and roasted him. The hen smelt the strong roast meat and sprung up to a higher peg and said, half-asleep, 'Faugh, what a nasty smell! What a nasty smell!' 'Oh stuff,' said the fox, 'it's only the smoke driven down the chimney; go to sleep again, and hold your tongue.'

So the hen went off to sleep again. Now the fox had hardly got the goose well down his throat before he did the same with the duck. He took and laid him on the embers and roasted him for a dainty bit. Then the hen woke up again, and sprung up to a higher peg still. 'Faugh, what a nasty smell! What a nasty smell!' she said again, and then she got her eyes open and came to see how the fox had eaten both the goose and the duck, so she flew up to the highest peg of all and perched there and peeped up through the chimney.

'O my; just see what a lovely lot of geese are flying yonder,' she said to the fox, and out ran Reynard to fetch himself another fat roast. But while he was gone, the hen woke up the cockerel and told him how it had gone with Goosey-Poosey and Ducky-Lucky; and so Cocky-Locky and Henny-Penny flew out through the chimney and if they hadn't got to Dovrefjell, it surely would have been all over with the world.

As it was not surely all over with us yet, on our own way to Dovrefjell. The commonest theme was not that things worked out but the ways in which things were solved – a magic mirror here, a comb there, an apple flung over the shoulder, a wisp of straw which allowed you to travel in an instant to the other side of the earth. It was always ingenuity, never strength. A fortuitous turn in the road, a dream shared by Henny-Penny, a lie told about a lovely lot of non-existent flying geese, a meeting with a photographer in the twilight, a passing on the stairs. I wasn't even going to have lunch that day, but a colleague persuaded me and the next thing I found myself standing in the refectory queue next to Marion.

We hardly touched, though occasionally as if to emphasise a point Helen would stroke the palm of my hand. Looking back on it now I'm aware of how non-sexual that evening was, yet electrified with expectation. I don't know whether that had to with age, though I suspect that had we been younger we would have forsaken sweetness for passion. And she was beautiful that evening in the firelight, the changing colours of the flames casting all kinds of wonderful shapes and contours on to her face and body. The way her cheekbones were framed best in the red, and how the last embers of each fire softened everything. And she said I too looked fine, stoking the stove.

We sang little songs to each other. Be kind to your web-footed friend, for the duck might be somebody's mother who lives all alone in a swamp where it's always cold and damp. You may think that's the end of the song; so it is, but I'll sing you another – I'll sing you the same one again, only this time a little higher... and off we'd go again, this time in a slightly higher pitch, until we eventually crumbled in fits of laughter like little children as the inevitable happened when we failed to reach the highest note of all which was beyond reach of anyone in the whole world when you came to think of it.

'What's the longest word you know?' she asked and of course I cheated and invented a long Gaelic word *agusnuairabhamiannanIlebhaCatrionacuideriumhoro* and then tried Mississippi and disestablishmentarianism and even resorted to supercaleygoballisticcelticareatrocious which was the best ever newspaper headline the morning after Inverness Caley Thistle had beaten the mighty Glasgow Celtic in the Scottish Cup, but we finally settled on Helen's word from childhood, *tikitikitembonosarembocharibaribuchipipperripembo*, which according to her was the name of a little Japanese boy in a story her mother used to tell her.

'Round and round the rugged rock the radical rascal ran' I tried, and she rattled it off with ease and gave me a variation which I struggled with for a while, 'round the rapid roundabout rolls the ripe and ready round brown prune', making it slightly more difficult for me by insisting that I then do it in a broad Scots accent, roond the raipid roondaboot rolls the raip and raidy roond broon proon. She said she should sit. And so she sat. And of course we always got the s and the h all mixed up, with the inevitable childish outcome.

Later on we got more serious. Mull, she said, was a microcosm. As in ecology, here was where you could see the future. I disagreed, of course, saying that human communities, being much more unpredictable and variable were not subject to the laws of science, but she just laughed at me saying that human society was as predictable as a hive of bees or a colony of ants. 'Change one thing and everything changes. And the changes become irreversible. This was once a Gaelic speaking island. Not any more. Once the hive is destroyed, the bees die.'

I wanted to argue otherwise of course: that there were hundreds of examples of reversal all over the world, from Hebrew to Catalan, but I knew these were straws in the wind. Science always heralded cosmology. Nothing will come of nothing. 'Though something might lead to something?' I suggested. The last log of wood was still burning in the fire. 'Of course,' she said. 'Where there's a flame there's a fire.'

My room was up in the attic: coombed and with v-lining and warmed now by the grate fire that we'd lit down below. I lay there, snug as the proverbial bug in the rug, thinking of young Alasdair, my grandfather, lying in a similar room almost a century before and racing with Nurmi. The touch which gave life to everything: stones which some mason had once hewn, the corrugated roof under which a family had sheltered, Helen moving about downstairs.

I switched off the bedside lamp and let the natural night light from outside illuminate the room. I tried to listen to rain running down the eaves, but there was none. In such a room as this the three of us had slept: myself and my two brothers. Everything lasted moments. The next thing nothing was there.

Things were scraping. A thin drizzle was now falling. I thought I heard some jazz, but the sound of a dog barking interrupted the music. A voice called. I recognised the voice: it was that man who'd given us the lift. Lachlan. So. I was in Mull. I went over to the small window and saw Helen leaving with Lachlan, whose collie dog jumped into the car first. They drove off.

I washed, dressed in the silk shirt and smock and old moleskin trousers I'd found in the chest, and went downstairs.

'Gone out with Lachlan on the boat,' the note read. 'Back this afternoon. Make yourself at home. H.'

No x. Always a good sign. It presumed nothing, demanded nothing. Things needed sorted, so I too left a note.

'Gone back to the mainland to return car. Then on to Paris to fix things up. Back soon.'

And I left my mobile number, just in case. I phoned Murdo the Taxi who took me to the ferry and by lunchtime was driving south.

I decided to take the peninsular road down through Kilmartin to Kintyre where I could catch the small Claonaig ferry on to Arran and from there the Brodick ferry to Ayrshire. I spent the night in Ardrossan where the ferry berthed, drove the car to York the next morning and by evening was back in our empty apartment by the Jardin.

I tried to phone Doctor Jacques, but there was no answer. He'd be away on his annual holiday up to the Nordic countries. 'Such a change of air from here,' he would say. 'Renews me for the rest of the whole year.'

I touched things, but they had no life. The flowers we'd left in the vase had obviously withered and though I went out to the corner shop to buy some more, the new ones still sat lifeless in the jar.

I played the piano for a while, and braced myself to enter our bedroom where she'd died. I felt nothing, except for a great emptiness as if nothing had ever happened. It wasn't an absence or a sense of loss, of something not being there, but of a vacancy in the air: a waiting for something rather than its departure.

I'd read that the first thing crash pilots do is to immediately return to the cockpit, so I opened the dressing room doors and put her blouses in order and stroked the collar of the fur coat which had become so un-PC as to be unwearable. I lay down on the bed. Our bed. She'd been on the left side, by the window, and I on the right side, by the door. I lay on my own side. Her diary was still opened by her bed, and I closed it.

The phone rang. Helen asked me how I was and I said 'Fine.'
'And you?'
'Good,' she said. 'Very good. Lachlan brought some fresh trout. They were lovely.'

She didn't ask if I planned to return to Scotland, and I didn't say, because I didn't know. After the call, I sat on the edge of the bed. The afternoon light streamed through the window – in this late summer time it filled the void between the two buildings opposite for about two hours, though in winter the sun never rose high enough to cast any light. The *mionagadain* danced in the air. I smiled. The word had come back to me just like that – a long forgotten thing that I'd never even thought about for years. The word for the atoms seen in a ray of sunlight coming into a house: *mionagadain.*

I tried to grab them, as I always did when I was young, and still failed. There was a secret to it though, my friend Angus had said. If you closed your eyes really tight and counted slowly to ninety-nine with both hands open and then suddenly shut the right one, you'd grab a handful of them before they got away.

So I started counting, my hands open as if in prayer. One two three four. The gap between each number had to be exactly the same, Angus had said. I got it wrong. I began again. One two three four. Still the beat was too quick. Too irregular.

'It has to be like this,' Angy said. 'One – breathe – two – breathe – three – breathe – four...' but of course when I got to the double figures I tripped up like a child and the rhythm went, and as any child knows, without rhythm the magic doesn't work.

I stood instead and walked through the atoms towards the window.

How beautiful Paris was in the late afternoon light. Someone was indeed playing jazz here: Stan Getz with that unmistakeable Indiana. Had I no feeling? My mind on childish atoms with my late wife newly scattered on the bare North Yorkshire Moors. Should my mind not be there, with her, or here in the rooms which we'd inhabited these past few years? Inhabited! Ha! Had the word betrayed me? Instead, I was elsewhere: always back in those days. And the miracle of Helen. No – perhaps more, just the miracle of meeting Helen. Of whom I knew so little. Was she too a figment of the imagination? One without flesh and blood, as if that really meant anything. One without substance, as if that in itself really meant anything either.

For weren't we all? That child I was. Once was, I was going

to say, but I paused. Hesitated. Am. The child that I am. That child who imagined he had a whole world in front of him. In which he would sail the seven seas, row the Atlantic single-handed, write a song greater than Kubla Khan, marry and have children and be a mirror image of his people. Or at least a mirror image of the best of his people. Those who'd fought valiantly at Inverkeithing, who hadn't turned back at Culloden, who had emigrated with the best of them, establishing the prairie fields of Canada and the sheep stocks of Patagonia. And here he was, that child, now an old man with thin hair and anaemic hands, looking out over Paris on an autumn afternoon. Ha! No one writes to the colonel.

By the time I turned back into the room the decision was taken. I phoned the lawyer and instructed her to oversee the selling of the apartment and the disposal of the furniture. Goods and chattels as they used to be called. I would leave with as little as possible, though that would still be far more than any of my ancestors ever had: Alasdair Mòr who'd emigrated to Australia with only a Bible in his pocket, and Caorstaidh Sheumais who bundled all her seven children on an empty cart and headed for Glasgow. They were all wearing National Health spectacles and whenever anyone asked if they'd seen the family, Lachie Mòr would say 'Last I saw was a cartload of spectacles heading south'.

I stayed a month altogether, ushering a number of potential buyers in through the apartment that first week, finally settling on selling it to a young Malaysian couple who were involved in setting up an organic clothing company. I phoned Helen and asked if I could come to Mull for a while and she said 'of course.' I doubt either of us will ever leave it.

10

'TO CELEBRATE,' SHE SAID, 'I went out with Lachlan on the boat last night, and thought you'd appreciate fresh sea trout after all these snails in Paris!'

We clinked glasses.

'*Slàinte.*'

What a strange thing love is. The notion that there you are, eighteen and head-over-heels, or that after a while it subsides, like a receding wave in the ocean. Those glorious stories once told about Romeo and Juliet and Deirdre and Naoise who, for the sake of love, went to their deaths. Like Christ too on Calvary. What was all this stuff about death and love? Love as Eros, as Philia, as Agape. And how in Gaelic you never really said 'I love you' but 'I like you'. *Is toigh leam thu.*

'Did you hear,' I asked her, 'about the Lewisman who loved his wife so much that he almost told her?'

And she laughed.

When she laughed, she had a dimple on one cheek. When the sun shone, as it did all that late autumn, freckles spread all over her face, like poppies on the machair. She grew her hair slightly longer, and was forever now flicking it behind her ears. It was just living next to the sea of course, but neither of us really realised how salty the air was until that first time we kissed. And it wasn't even by the sea, but inland up beyond the old Gruline sheep fank the day we decided to climb Beinn a' Ghràig.

We descended in the evening by the western shore of Loch Bà and spent some time standing there looking west out towards Eòrsa, Inch Kenneth and Ulva when we just turned towards each other, smiled and kissed. It only lasted moments, then we separated, and laughed.

'Look at us,' she said.

'Aye. Just look at us,' I answered and then we kissed properly, as we wanted to, without caution or fear.

'*Saillte*,' I said.

'More salt in the air here than there is in the Red Sea itself,' she said, smiling. 'And remember I know – I'm an Ecologist!'

That night Helen played the violin for the first time in my presence. She tuned it with part of Vivaldi's *Allegro*, which I recognised, then played the wonderful *Serenata* by Stravinsky and finished with a piece I didn't know.

'The *Pavano-Capricho* by Isaac Albeniz,' she said. 'I played it once upon a time for my Grade 8.'

'No one plays like that just from once upon a time. What about any fiddle tunes?' I asked.

'They were lost with the instrument. Except,' she said, putting the violin down on the table, 'that the case turned up a wee while back. Just before you turned up.'

I raised my hands in protest.

'It wisnae me!'

There was a thing I never quite understood.

'So,' I asked her. 'What's the difference between a fiddle and a violin anyway?'

'One makes music,' she said. 'The other plays it. It's your job to work out which does what.'

'And this one here?' I asked, pointing to the violin on the table.

'Here,' she said, handing it to me. 'Work it out.'

I raised the bow to the strings and tried to remember the few tunes I'd learned on the accordion as a child, but the scratches I made bore no resemblance to the almost forgotten sound inside my head.

'I'm afraid this one neither makes nor plays music,' I said. 'And this fiddle you lost?'

'It was in the family. Belonged to the family.'

'And made great music?'

'Yes. It made great music.'

'And – and are you telling me that you can't play... I mean make... fiddle music on this violin?'

'Yes. At least I can't.'

'And the case?'

'I saw it at a railway station. Just months ago. Crianlarich Railway Station, to be exact.'

She walked over to the cupboard by the fire. She took out a card and gave it to me.

'JULIE STONE' the card read. 'TRINITY ROAD, EDINBURGH', with a website and mobile number.

'Of course she was not the one who stole it – my God, it was almost fifty years ago now. But it was the case. Who knows that the fiddle itself might not miraculously appear in the same way?'

'I suppose you asked her?'

'What? If the poor child was playing a once-upon-a-time stolen fiddle? Hah! But I made sure it wasn't – she was just playing a poor shadow of a kind of thing.'

'But you got her address, just in case?'

'She told me she'd got the case from an old junk man who lived near her. I thought it might be fun one fine day just to go and see him...'

'You want me to phone?'

'No. I'll email her myself. Tell her I lied.'

'Lied?'

'Yes. I wanted her address so I could then get the old man's. The only reasonable way I thought of getting it at the time was to tell her that sometimes I held ceilidhs and she could maybe play at one of them...'

'Well we do, don't we?'

She smiled. 'Yes. I suppose we do.'

We travelled down to Edinburgh on the Monday. Held hands as we walked off the platform: all foolishness was permitted in the city. Julie herself came to meet us at Waverley and Helen just told her the truth: showed her the place where the station bench had been, once upon a time, and how she'd stood and turned, then turned back to find her fiddle gone.

'So this old junk man,' she said. 'I thought it might be worth my while seeing him, just in case he had any idea where that case he gave you came from in the first place.'

Julie gave us the address.

'He's a wonderful old guy. Completely eccentric. Maybe even mad? But a fantastic musician – can play any and all of the thousand bits of instruments he has in that yard of his. Oh, and he's a bit deaf too. Or at least pretends to be: sometimes he doesn't hear the clearest thing you say to him, but then demands silence and asks you to listen and sure enough you too will then hear it – a bird singing somewhere far above his garden. His name's Isaac. Jewish, of course.'

He was just off the 23 bus route, down a vennel where a small garage had once operated, which had now been converted into a domestic town house. Iron railings then led down beside the stream which took us to the bottom of his allotment where an old stile opened into the garden. Julie led the way, having been in and out of the yard since early childhood.

I can't really remember, but it must have taken us at least half-an-hour to finally find Isaac himself, resting in a hammock swung between his kitchen awning and a lovely old pine tree. On the way Julie stopped us time and again to show us bits of instruments which lay in nooks and crannies all over the place – xylophones and glockenspiels and horns and organs and bits of flutes and piccolos and half a celesta along with a thousand and one other bits and pieces which only God himself could recognise.

Isaac looked down at us from his hammock.

'Ah! My dear Juliette,' he said. 'And you bring visitors?'

'Indeed I do, Mr Stein.'

'Musicians too?' he asked.

'Of course. Of course they are.'

'Good. Good. Tell them to look around. Tell them to take their time. We have all the time in the world.'

And he closed his eyes and lay back down in his hammock again.

Inside, the house was just as full of objects as the yard outside. Sets of bagpipes, including Athertons and old Glens and MacDougalls side by side with harmonicas and sections of saxophones. Mounds of sheet music of course as well as old LPs which were a connoisseur's dream.

And there it was. Down on the floor, half obscured behind a pile of suitcases which were filled with trumpets and trombones, beneath a broken down harpsichord.

Helen didn't say anything: just knelt down, removing some of the sheet music which had fallen on top of it: *Chanson dans le Nuit*, by Carloz Salzedo. Not that it matters, except that it's one of those maddening details I remember, as she flung it aside.

Her index finger swept all the dust off the scroll and then she just knelt there in silence staring down at the instrument.

She lifted it, tenderly, and all the lost myths of time were in that embrace. It was the prodigal son and the lost sheep and the lost coin and Jason and the Golden Fleece and Long John Silver with fifteen men on the dead man's chest. Drink and the devil had done for the rest.

She laughed.

'Ha! X never marks the spot! O, yes it does!'

She lifted the fiddle up and brushed all the dust off with a corner of her shirt and laughed again.

'Now all I need is a bow.'

Julie and I of course bowed down.

'There's some, over there' said Julie, climbing over bits of a nickelodeon to where several bows lay in a glass cabinet. She opened the cabinet and took one out and gave it to Helen, who spent the next half hour or so trying to tune the fiddle.

'It needs a new E string,' she said, so back to the glass cabinets where a whole host of strings were piled on different shelves. She finally found one and the fiddle sounded magnificent. A deliverance was in the air.

She eventually took it through to Isaac who by now was sitting up in a grand wicker chair drinking tea from a wonderful old urn.

'This fiddle, Sir. Can you remember where it came from?'

The old man looked intently at the fiddle for a while then said, 'Could I try it out?'

She handed it to him and he raised it to his right cheek and began to play left-handed. An exquisite sound came from the instrument as we all stood there listening to the whole violin concerto which he finished with the quietest fioritura any of us had ever heard. He handed the violin back to Helen and said.

'Yours. As a gift.'

Unfortunately, I broke the spell.

'The lady wondered where the instrument came from in the first place,' I said to him.

He smiled and spread out his hands.

'Don't we all wonder that? It belongs to the whole world. To everyone.'

He swept his outspread hands round the yard and the house.

'These things. They belong to you. Private ownership has no place in music. No music, no instrument belongs to a single individual.'

I could have protested. But this fiddle – this violin – belonged to her anyway. Belonged to her family in the first place, to that Archibald Campbell who'd bought it in Naples and brought it here initially. Was stolen from her. Isaac smiled at us.

'Isn't everything stolen? From God. Our lives are not our own. Will I not restore unto you the years that the locust hath eaten?'

We accepted his gift, considering the lost years as a thing lent, rather than sold.

I I

WHEN SHE WORKED in Ireland Helen learned how to weave.
Down Connemara way it was, in a village near Spideal where
she'd been sent by the environmental department to assess the
ecological damage that the emerging fish-farming industry
might cause to the inland lochs. She roomed at the hotel for
the first month or so but then managed to get a little cottage to
rent out in the country and had the great good fortune to find
herself next door to Máire Cassidy who had woven the golden
fleece for Father Patrick Mahoney when he left with half his
congregation between the wars for Australia.

She was ninety when Helen met her, one Saturday afternoon
as she cycled out in the country. That rock-filled area of
Connemara where the wild horses graze over the stone walls.
Helen came round a corner and almost struck the old woman
down as she crossed the road. She managed to stop in time. The
old woman looked at her and smiled and continued across the
single-track road, climbed a small wooden stile and began to
move towards a wooden shed sitting by the river. She beckoned
Helen to follow her, so Helen lay her bike down by the roadside,
climbed the stile and followed her down to the river's edge.

The weaving shed had originally been the family home before
her father gathered all the stones to build the little cottage where
she now stayed. It was turf-roofed with two little windows to
the front and a tiny window to the back. It took Helen a long

time to become acquainted with the dark, which was not really dark at all once you became used to it. A kerosene lamp hung over the table where all the wools lay in bundles, and through the small shafts of sunlight she could make out various tables and hooks and spindles hanging on the walls. She could hear the old woman moving things in the dark: was that a handle turning, and a desk opening, and castanets rattling?

Then she heard the unmistakable sound of the thread on the loom and the levers being ploughed and the clickity-clack of the wool being spun. A sound from far away which was actually next to her once her eyes adjusted to the light. That old-fashioned kind of spinning-wheel which now only lived in photographs. The old left hand ceaselessly fed the thread as the right hand twirled and the wool cascading in rings down into the dark on the far side.

And the old woman began to talk. 'Sure and it's a wonder to people all right but what's to be wondered at after all wouldn't you say the way the world is and don't I know it what with having had Geraldine and Mairead and Sean and Bernadette and Patrick as if I didn't know the way it is the wonder of it is that it has lasted so long and not a day that something doesn't need to be done and is done.'

She spoke like the spinning wheel, in threads. 'Memory! Memory they say the beesoms as if they knew anything about memory and that woman who comes by and tells me I'm losing mine as if there was anything to lose in the first place because it's all got to with living, hasn't it after all my dear, is what I said to her. You see – the wool is put here in your left palm my dear and then it runs clear through the spindle and all the little crinkles and cronkles and crankles are straightened out and of course if you want to mix it with other wool to make different colours well you just do that like this so that what it has been matters less than what it will be.'

And she lifted three other balls of wool in her left hand and began to feed the different colours simultaneously through the wheel. Then she laughed. 'Memory!' She looked directly at

Helen for the first time, and Helen smiled. And the old woman smiled.

'My name is Máire Cassidy,' she said. 'I'm now ninety years of age and still spin here every day except for the Sunday. Do you know that everything has a memory, this wool included, maybe especially this wool which remembers the sheep it kept warm and the way that bitter February wind once tugged at it and that time poor old Seumas got stuck in the barbed wire when he tried to untangle me and it's the devil's own work to tray and untangle all that memory because it curls up where it wishes until you uncurl it and loops when it shouldn't and you want it straight but I've worked out ways to treat that by treading it through this other machine here on the floor which makes sure that all the wool is nice and straight and flat and long except of course when you want it curled and handsome.' She looked up at Helen again. 'The important thing, my darling, is not to hide the future. Sheep don't they know this is their future, this jumper I'm making which I'll send to young Sean for when he goes to the hurling; in the same way they make such fine chops despite what that old bugger Maloney claims with all that rittle rattle he gibbers about flux and bluetongue as if we didn't know how to separate the sheep from the goats and didn't know a good hind leg when we saw one who were raised on mutton and milk and none of that plastic flim-flam he sells for a guinea as if he was selling you the queen's breast.'

The wool was making a terrific pattern in her hands: white and blue and brown and green. She laughed too. 'None of it happens by magic despite what they think all that baloney about leprechauns and *sìth-sha-sìth* unless you get the tangles out straightaway otherwise it's all messed up and nothing leads to nothing, just like old Meg along the road who tried to make a pair of trousers for Bert which ended up as the dog's rug out in the porch and not the first or the last time either.'

How tempting it was to leave and dismiss the ramblings of the old, but she stayed. All afternoon, listening to the endless weaving of Máire's words until she began to make sense of them. As with everything else. She was an amateur. Knew nothing really about knitting or spinning or weaving, and how one thing led to another, depended upon something else. The better the ground was tilled and the better it was manured and mulched the better the grass grew, and how it was always better to rotate the crops and fields so that sheep would be there one year and horses the next and cows the next and goats the next though sometimes all together and the better you did that the better the grass was and the better the grass was the better the sheep fed and the better their chops were and their wool which would be fine and coarse and fluffy, and how you kept the sheep clean from lice and keds and worms and weeds and how the Cotswolds are better than the Blackface and that was before you went anywhere near the clipping and shearing and spinning itself.

Which she did, for the whole five years she was there, spending every Saturday with Máire Cassidy in her wooden shed. At first listening and watching, then sitting down beside her and letting Máire's ancient hand guide hers through the knotted wool, kneading it this way and that on the stave, then letting her hand lie in Máire's as she pounded the wool on the trestle, then learning how to pick up the crotal from the hill rocks and how to mix that with the dye from the water-lilies so as to give unknown colours to the wool before threading it through the ancient spindles, woofing and warping, all the way through to sitting knitting by the stove, Máire on one side and Helen on the other, making scarves and bobble-hats and stockings and jerseys stitch by knot, inch by yard, one after the other.

It was during these five years in Ireland that she met Feargal. Feargal the Jockey whose most famous victory was on Autumn Gold at the St Leger. She met him that first summer when he was home for a few days for his grandfather's funeral. Helen was out walking the moors on the Sunday afternoon when this white vision appeared on the horizon – something moving backwards and forwards on the high slopes. The further she climbed she realised it was a white horse moving with wonderful speed and elegance, jumping the dykes, leaping the little river-streams which began up there near the scree. The horse and rider stopped and stood still watching her and waiting for her arrival.

He was a young man, wearing an Aran jersey – how well she knew the names and types by now! – and a cowboy hat. He waved to her and she waved back and went straight up to the horse and began stroking its mane. She'd always had a way with horses from her childhood in Mull. The silly little ponies which nuzzled in by the old fank walls and then Bess the old mare who loved running through the sea at the world's edge. And this beautiful looking horse stood still in the breeze, whinnying as she stroked the mane down beyond the neck.

He asked her if she'd like to go for a canter and she said aye and he stretched out his hand and she leapt up behind him, holding him fast across the waist. He had beautiful wrists which turned the horse this way and that with the tiniest movement and a way of delicately controlling the horse as it approached all obstacles. She could sense the fractional slowing down as the river came, then the minimal tightening of the rein before the great leap, and then the steady run across the moor before leaping the old stone dykes, through the gaps on the way out, and over the very highest part of the walls on the way back.

'I can do it myself, of course' she said to him and he handed her the reins and off she went across the moorland. The horse rode itself: it slowed down when approaching the rivers, then leapt, galloped freely across the moorland, found the lowest part of the dykes on the way out and the highest parts on the way back. 'So,' she said to him, 'the magic is in the horse? As always.' He smiled. 'Aye, but it's not learned overnight.'
He worked at the famous Curragh stables in Kildare and was one of the very few who rode professionally in both flat and jumps races. 'This is the best training in the whole wide world,' he said. 'Leaping the rivers and dykes, racing across the moors. And this is my favourite horse – she's called Eachbàn.' He

whistled and a chestnut horse came galloping over the ridge. 'And this is Eachruadh, her friend. Yours while you're here.'

They rode side by side down the hill.

These years in Ireland were an eternal moment. There was no forward planning, and no backward looking. Just being alive, day after day. The delight of waking in the morning all cooried up in the cottage bed, and lighting the fire – always the same small struggle to clean out the ashes – ach, why didn't I do it last thing at night – then the careful placing of the kindlers and the sparking of the match which lit the *Irish Times* and caught the wood as you closed the stove door and washed yourself in the makeshift shower and prepared breakfast. And the amazing drive out through the rocky landscapes to the loughs where the fish-cages were, and the rowing out into the middle of the lake, and the afternoons spent in that sunny lab upstairs making sure all things were right, and then sometimes the evening session down at the local pub, and the increasing day trips to Kildare to meet up with Feargal, and then every Saturday the endless learning and weaving with Máire Cassidy.

One night as they lay in bed Feargal said, 'I don't believe in the white horse any more.' She had the sense to remain quiet. 'You see,' he said, 'the old people all said they'd seen it. Or at least some of them said they had. Or had heard of folk who said they had. My dad told me he had seen it himself. Up there on the high ridge at the back of the mountain, one morning as he was coming back from herding the cattle. Said he just glanced up and there it was standing high with its forelock up into the sky on what we call here A' Chreig Mhòr – The Great Rock. He approached it and of course when he got nearer the steed turned east and galloped off towards the Sliabh.'

She just knew. 'And what about you? Did you ever see it yourself?'

He lit a cigarette.

'Shouldn't be smoking them, of course, but it keeps the weight down. Yes.'

'Where?'

'Everywhere. The first time when I was about three and I was playing over by the old well. The white horse suddenly appeared, as if from nowhere, and took a drink out of the big tin bucket that was swinging there on the pump handle. Drank it all then galloped off over the stone walls. Then when I was seven, just after my confirmation. We'd come back from mass and I was out with a bat trying to play rounders over in the in-field when he appeared on the roof of the old barn, whinnying. By the time I ran over he'd disappeared. But the best time was when I was thirteen. I was out with the dog on the moor between the old mill and the school when I saw him standing grazing quietly in the green pasture. I ordered the dog to lie still and walked slowly and gently up to him and smoothed his mane and patted him and led him over to the wall where I mounted. That was the morning I learned to be a horseman. He led all the way.'

He stopped, as if that was the end of thought. Helen stroked the back of his hand.

'And then?'

'And then I became a horseman.' He laughed. 'A jockey. Hiring myself out to race. For gamblers.

'But there's far more to it than that,' she said. 'I've seen you, been with you there, Feargal. Your passion for the sport, for the spectacle, for the beasts themselves. You love them, they're so beautiful and athletic and brave.'

It felt like a speech and she regretted it.

'Give it up then. Return back home to Connemara.'

'I can't. Because I don't believe in the white horse any more.'

'Why not?'

Which is when he hesitated, like a little boy.

'Because nobody else does. It was just a dream. Something I imagined.'

As if that mattered. As if everything wasn't imagined. She kissed him. And afterwards,

'Did you imagine that?'

But it was too late. Other people's opinions mattered too much to him, had already frittered away his belief. And her love was not devotion or salvation. She knew that not even sharing the haycorn plain and purl speech of Máire Cassidy, with all its fun and runs, could rescue him from the fall. That required far more than human touch and liquid language. The thing was that he had grown accustomed to the race. To winning. That rush of adrenalin as he whipped horse through the final furlong and crossed the line, a hand raised in triumph. Had become accustomed to the thrill of gambling – that uncertainty, unless it was fixed, that this time the outsider would romp home at 12/1. It wasn't about the white horse any more but about winning, at any cost.

What choice did Judas have? That night he went out into the dark, and took the thirty pieces of silver, and kissed Jesus to betray him. When he went out to hang himself. Or the innkeeper, for after all, the motel was full. And young Pontius himself, for after all what else could a man in his position do except wash his hands of the whole affair? O, for a thousand tongues to sing my great Redeemer's praise! O, for the faith to believe that all was possible, that dark could turn to light, drunkenness to sobriety, this to that. That man could walk on the moon and that as shepherds watched their flocks by night all seated on the ground the angel of the Lord came down and glory shone all round.

Old Murdina always used to say, '*An car a bhios anns an t-seanna mhaide, 's duilich a thoirt às*' – the twist that is in the old stick is not easily made straight – which didn't prevent her from believing with all her heart, soul, mind and strength that no one was beyond redemption and that the worst of sinners always made the best of saints. Though even divine love itself failed where folk kept making the wrong choices. But isn't it a miracle that we recognized Him when He called.' she always added.

After she broke up with Feargal she rediscovered the joy of independence. What it was really like to be liberated from hope and ambition, free from regret and disappointment. How almost impossible it was just to be yourself. She had a week's holiday and spent it in Dublin. Cut her hair first thing on Monday morning. Short, though not in tribute. That was to be someone else. To be a fan or an acolyte. She stayed on the south side, out near Bray, and walked on the strand for a while and visited Martello Tower and into town of course to wander around Temple Bar and St Stephen's Green to see the statues and the busts. She lay there on the grass for a while looking up at the cloudless sky and realised that she could remember everything that had ever happened because none of it was a memory but a film before her eyes. The cow and the blackbird and the bicycle and the lad who had passed her on the stairs and the way Feargal O'Shaughnessy turned his wrists to steer the horse. None of it had happened once upon a time because it was happening now, like Máire Cassidy's yarn spinning on to the whorl spindle, erasing and making memory, turning a sheep's fleece into a little girl's scarf.

Later on that day she took the Dart train south to Howth and there on Claremont Beach looked into the mirror the other way round. All statements are ridiculous in the arms of your lover, where all that matters is truth and touch. The breakers were pounding against the far skerries, where Feargal was already swimming towards the incoming tide. For what shall it profit a man if he shall gain the whole world and lose his soul? He would become a prize-fighter in the light welterweight divisions, but the punches would take their toll, and the pub was the inevitable outcome, where those who stayed got equal share in the spoils with those who fought. She loved him too much to share that with him in the end.

She stood naked in front of the hotel's full-length mirror that last morning of her week in Dublin. The short dark hair curling upwards at the edges, the fine blades of her shoulders, the tiny birth-mark just above the left hip. How little your body revealed of your soul. The possibility of prostituting everything, for what? Food to turn to fat, a salary, a career, a family? And the possibility of denying it all, as if these breasts couldn't milk, as if love didn't matter. Like everyone else, she'd have to wait and see. For who could mastermind anything, who could calibrate the future? She was twenty-five years of age.

She caught the bus back to Connemara that afternoon. An old country bus which took her down through Kildare and on to Port Laoise and through parts of North Tipperary, in the olden days before Eireann too became one big highway where you travelled quick and straight. They passed tractors on the road and here and there saw the occasional haystack and the endless roadside shrines and grottoes.

Back home she lit the fire and cycled down to see Máire who made her some tea in the old pot, then read the leaves for her when she'd finished. 'There's a cross and a flag and a daisy,' she said, 'though I shouldn't be telling you these secrets except what they mean as if an old biddy could see one thing and say another for it all hangs on what you see in the first place but no matter what others would see it's not them who's seeing it but me and I've been seeing it so long now that I know more what things are not than what they are which means that what I see is what it is because the other things don't matter at all and would just spoil it and get in the way of the only thing that matters which is making sense of them so that the cross is hard-won happiness and the flag is danger and the daisy is love and they will all happen except all these white bits on the cup – do you see them? – are unknown and only the good Lord Himself can reveal these in His own good way in His own good time for all I do is just look at where the leaves lie and have faith in the rest my dear there is nothing like love and never let anything fame or power or money or pain or anything else kill it,' she said.

That all happened a long time ago, though Helen hadn't just remembered it all of a sudden, out of the blue. How could one ever forget that haphazard way of speaking, as if running across cobblestones or walking fast in the moonlight because if a sheep coughed it sounded so much like a dead man waking in Pennygown cemetery which made you aware of nothing and a thousand things at once? Who was it who said that the language of the fool is the language of the devil, in other words of the *other*, of what has been expelled, suppressed, repressed, oppressed and beaten? Who had language for any of it?

The moon was shining down on them as they drove back through Mull. Its liquid light poured down from the mountains and across the sea leaving a perfection reflection of itself in the loch. And the shapes inside the moon! The dark cheese portions, and look there's grampa's beard and granny's big round wire specs and before you knew it a man was jumping all over it and bouncing up and down on it except that old Archie said they'd never land that way on the sun, though he was silenced by Morag who told him that of course they would, but during the night when the fire was out and it was cold.

And there now on the far side of the loch was their little stone cottage, where they would soon light the fire and have supper.

12

THE TV IMAGES were just too harrowing for comfort. We'd returned from a day out at the Tobermory Games and had switched the telly on to find ourselves back in a world which we'd pretended had ceased to exist. The flies around the swollen eyes always wrenched the heart, and this time, half a century on from Biafra, was no different. That in itself only prompted the conscience.

Then the email came from the government's Disaster Emergency Committee – invariably known by its acronym as the DEC – asking if she'd consider coming out of early retirement to lead one of the UNICEF-led water development programmes in the Horn of Africa. They couldn't as yet tell the exact location until continuing negotiations with some of the local Islamic organisations unfolded, but if that worked out as they hoped, it would be in Somalia.

I wanted to go with her but she persuaded me to stay at home, forcibly arguing that years of experience had taught her that the worst thing that could happen would be for goodwilled amateurs like me to start interfering in things.

'Just stay near the cash machine,' she said to me as she left.

'That and on your knees praying. These are two best places from which to send aid.'

She left at the beginning of our winter. It was one of the most severe winters on record. Snow began to fall in early November, and hardly ceased until the May of the following year. At first we considered it a joke, and the occasional messages we managed to send to each other were peppered with weather references.

'Could do with your snow here in Mogadishu.'

'A bit of that Somalian sunshine would go down just grand here in Salen,' but in time the reality in both places removed us beyond jokes.

The brutal combination of famine and heat continued to bring daily death to Africa, while here on Mull the endless months of rain and snow caused landslides, blocked roads, frozen pipes, flooding and a severe crisis which brought its own death toll, with accounts of old folk on the peninsula frozen in their unheated homes.

Of course we knew that it was all relative, but the death of Lachlan who was caught in a snowstorm out on the moor whilst looking for his sheep made it very real for both of us on both sides of the globe.

By Easter a reasonable thaw had set in here, while even better news came from Africa: the long awaited rains had finally arrived and a steadiness had set in which gave people hope.

Helen managed to phone from the local hospital saying that she would now also stay on for the summer as they now had a proper chance to set up a water system in the area she was working in, which should be in operation by the end of September. Rival politicans were trying to talk to one another.

'I'll be home for the local Mod,' she said. 'You know how much the Mull choir rely on my dulcet tones!'

'I think I'll travel out,' I said to her, and I let her protest vehemently for a while before interrupting to say 'I mean travel out to Uist. To see some of the old haunts, for the summer. After all, I'm here on my own, and you won't be back until...'

'October,' she interrupted. And the line went dead.

I travelled west on the first day in July. It was a glorious Monday morning with the sun already high in the sky above distant Ben Cruachan as we sailed out of Oban where my mother had worked in the hotels, as a kitchen maid. The Great Western. The Royal. The Regent. She always prayed that the guests would leave her a tip. Then one summer Kirk Douglas came and stayed for a week. He left behind his slippers and she took them home for us to try them on. They were grey and far too big for any of us and became lost to history. And there's the old pier where the fish factory was where she shelled the prawns. And the railway station Refresh where we'd wait for the bus while old Dougie sang *An t-Eilean Muileach*. And old Mrs MacFarlane always gave us a florin.

I stand up on the foredeck to make sure I can see everywhere. The time since I'd last stood here. At least forty years ago. No. Don't be such a fool. Work it out exactly. It won't take that much effort. Just count. Face up to it. Forty-seven years then. Forty-seven years since I'd last stood here as a young student, Kilchoan and Beinn Seilg and Ardnamurchan Point to my right, Sorisdale and Rudha Sgor-innis and Eilean Mòr and Rudha Mòr to my left. What I believed then. Being and Nothingness by Jean-Paul Sartre. Stevie Wonder was on the turntable. The fragrant smell of marijuana as we marched against Vietnam. When everything that was so value-laden seemed so value-free, including J-P himself who turned out, after all, just to be another womaniser hiding his lust behind scholarship.

I wish I had an Admiralty Chart so that I could track every rock and skerry, every bay and inlet. Look – there's Rubha Shamhnan and Rubha na Mòine and Rubha na h-Iolaire, and look – over there's Sgùrr an Easain Duibh and Sgùrran Seilich, and if you look backwards you can just see the peak of Sgùrr Eachainn disappearing over the horizon. But of course I know them more generally, for that – despite the fact that in the meantime Bombay has become Mumbai and Rhodesia has become Zimbabwe – has not changed.

See – there's Moidart and Ardnamurchan and up yonder is Muck and Eigg and Rum and Canna and over by is Coll and Tiree, and ahead of course is Miùghlaigh and Barraigh and Èirisgeigh and Uibhist-a-Deas. Like Mumbai, Moidart is of course Mùideart and like Zimbabwe, Ardnamurchan is really Àird nam Murchain which, if translatable at all, 'means' something like 'The High Place of the Sea-hounds, or Otters'.

I don't know anyone on the ferry and, as far as I can make out, no one knows me. How things have changed. I look at faces to see if I can see the children of the children of children I once knew, and I suspect I do. Isn't that Donald the Post over there crouched over his laptop, and isn't that Catriona, famous for riding her horse bareback across the heather, drinking coffee and yattering away on her mobile. I nod at people and they nod back in courtesy.

We are now in the open seas: that part of the exposed Minch you get once you leave the relative shelter of Tiree and head west. This was always the time in the old days to put the head down and batten the hatches as you lay there battered by force eight winds which flung everything into space. Plates flew and doors creaked and you could hear the anchor chains crying, and then babies bawled and men spewed and someone was always drunk and singing in the bar while an endless accordion tune wailed behind him. You woke in the dark to find the vessel still being tossed about, and surrounded by the stale smell of vomit, despite the efforts of the cabin crew to mop up. I close my eyes now in the calm of the new digitally enhanced ship and can still smell the chaos and the fear.

And upstairs – or was it downstairs? – was where the first-class lounge was and the white-clothed tables where the well-to-do dined from bow-tied waiters, while we languished next to the cattle in the steerage. O my God, I'd almost forgotten that – the sight of lifting cows and cars on to harnesses into the boat at Lochboisdale pier and then the pitiful sounds they made during the long crossing as the swell rose and fell and the waves thumped against the prow.

I remember once sneaking into the first-class dining room on some kind of lying pretext and managing to get a plate of food away with me. It was a salad – the first time I'd ever seen one. Two thick slices of the best cold ham were covered in a white sauce and next to it things I'd never seen before which I now believe to have been tomatoes and asparagus and rocket and lettuce. I smuggled them down to my father in the steerage who took one look at the plate and said,

'Do you think I'm a cow or something?'

He came to my graduation, which was a rather grand affair in the Sheldonian Theatre. I didn't want to go of course – considered it a bourgeois pretence, but since my parents had worked and struggled so hard to make sure I was educated, I felt at the time that at least we ought to have a day out.

I remember once when I was very young – it must have been during the time of what they called the Eleven Plus exam – my father walked ten miles through the rain to the house of the local council clerk so that he could borrow his fountain pen for me for the day of the examination.

I sat at the small northerly window in our hut for hours waiting for him to return and I can still see him in his big green raincoat coming over the hill a mile or so to the north. I still remember the fountain pen, which was red with a blue top and which squirted ink everywhere once you dipped it into the inkwell which he'd also acquired.

'No no no no – don't waste it,' he shouted, and my fun was spoilt. Only two of us passed the Eleven Plus: myself and the local harbour master's son, George, who later became a professor, and the last I heard of him he was teaching at the Massachusetts Institute of Technology.

The graduation, which took place on a hot day in June, was rather like a cattle market. These would happen twice a year, the spring sales and the autumn sales, when men and women would drag a bellowing cow by a rope down the main road, to be sold to the drovers.

We would sit by the roadside shouting insults at them, 'There you go Seumas – you'll get a ha'penny for that one!' 'You'd be as well going back home with that one – the drovers will think you're trying to sell a mouse!'

The further you travelled with your cow the less chance you had: the drovers knew fine it was too long to travel back in the dark with a reluctant cow and would offer ha'pennies towards the end of the day for the poor beasts. 'There goes poor Peggy with her sixpence,' my mother would say.

Old Seònaid made a fine name for herself. There she was at the end of the day dragging her only cow round the auction ring. We listened open-mouthed as the auctioneer began his magic incantations: the cattle rattle acaramaarabid abaracadaabin which we later understood to mean hundred-for-a-bid, hundred-for-a-bid, ninety-for-a-bid, ninety-for-a-bid... and on reaching the halfway low point of fifty-for-a-bid with not one single hand raised old Seònaid was heard to protest, 'S e a' bhò a tha mi reic 's chan e an ròpa' –' 'It's the cow I'm selling, not the rope!'

For the graduation, we all hired ridiculous gowns from somewhere and then sat in preapportioned rows and moved forward one row at a time as our disciplines and classes were called. I'd almost persuaded my father to hire a kilt for the day but he refused point blank saying that he'd rather go naked than dress up in that stuff. I almost called his bluff, but knowing that he would do it, backed down, only because I knew they would restrain him at the door if he arrived nude. So he too hired a suit and sat ill at ease at the back, but proud enough to see one of the family, for the first time ever, getting a university degree, which are now so two-a-penny.

Afterwards, we went for what used to be called High Tea then, to The White Horse Inn on Broad Street, which was at the time run by a rather jolly couple from Edinburgh. A three-course graduation special was on, which seemed reasonable value – lentil soup, followed by stew and potatoes, and then apple pie with custard. I smile now, about the innocence of these pre-health-choice, pre-salad days. You'll have had your tea? Afterwards I think we went to a pub, though we wouldn't have stayed long for my father didn't drink and then I took him back to his lodgings which were on the other side of All Soul's. It was the last time he was ever on the mainland.

Those Oxford years were an adventure, and looking back on them I don't think I've ever properly removed myself from them. I've always been eighteen, and expecting the Rowing Club boys to come round any moment to head out on one of our wild escapades. Richard even had a Bentley in the third year, which of course was a great attraction when it came to women. The Mark VI Sports Saloon, which was the one with the all-steel body and the 4.6 litre engine.

Most Sundays were spent driving round the Cotswolds: up to Stratford-upon-Avon to the North, and the beautiful city of Bath to the south. The names still ring like childhood rhymes in my head, and I can still see Richard, with his long scarf, and myself and Jodie and Lucy singing our hearts out as we drank champagne through these ancient places overwhelmed by tourists like ourselves – Bourton-on-the-Water, Burford, Chipping Norton, Salisbury, Stow-on-the-Wold. How big and pretty the thatched cottages out there were, like little story-book castles, compared to the ones I knew.

And punting, with its inevitable rhyme! How I scoffed at first until I tried it and then realised that, like everything else, it was not as simple as it looked. What I couldn't really stand were the boat races themselves, with these ever-so-keen athletes, in their eights and sculls and coxless fours and all the rest. Too many public schoolboys for my liking, though I have to confess I liked a whole bunch of them including Richard who had been through Eton, but was as full of earthy fun and joy as anyone I've ever met.

He was a wonderful climber, with a whole number of first ascents to his credit which still stand in the record books. He was the first to ice-climb the north peak of the Cryther Pass in Snowdonia and has several similar credits to his name in the Alps. I agreed to go climbing with him once to Glencoe, when he ascended both the North Buttress and the Crowberry Ridge alongside the great Scottish climber Dougal Haston.

I tried the first bit with them, but pulled out when I froze with fear about one-third of the way up, even though I was well harnessed to both. Richard was also a great musician – a flautist – latterly playing with the London Philharmonic before retiring to Australia where his partner's son and daughter live.

The ferry is sailing smoothly through the waters. I will stay in a hotel on my home island for the first time in my life. Mostly because I don't really have any close relatives left whom I feel I know well enough to stay with, but also through choice – it will give me more independence and freedom of movement without having to explain anything to anyone, except maybe to myself. Does that make me selfish? Are my cousins and my second cousins once or twice removed not entitled to share my life before I share it with the world? Am I entitled even to do share it with myself? The world. The little big big little big little world. Someone scores a goal on the television. Ronaldo. Whatever happened to Alan Gilzean?

The sailing into Lochboisdale harbour is as charming as it always was. The lighthouse at Calvay greets us again and the pier lights are as welcome as they always were. How few people now meet the ferry. Where once the quay was thronged – the arrival of the ferry was such a great event – is now a great emptiness. Because mobile phones are not permitted on the car deck folk sit silently in their cars waiting to drive off, while those coming on board for the outgoing sailing play with their iPhones or their radios.

I walk up to the pier hotel and find myself, for the first time ever, in the upstairs quarters of a mysterious world. Downstairs in the bar they used to have great bare-knuckle fights as in the westerns. When I was young I came to the hotel twice – once for a wedding reception when I was about seven and once again some years after for a meal after a funeral. In those days, this hotel belonged to the gentry and only those of a certain age and means – mainly men on a fishing holiday – stayed here. And here I was now, of that age, and of those means.

The young woman at reception has no idea I belong to the place and welcomes me with warmth and with grace, and even gives me advice about the attractions of the area and some of the places I should visit.

'The beaches are great,' she says, 'and of course if you want to go fishing, we can arrange for a local gillie to take you to some of the best lochs and rivers.'

I pause on the stairs on the way up to my room to admire the wonderful catches that famous fishermen have made over the years, with the stuffed fish now encased in glass cages. How I'd admired these that time I came for the wedding reception: I don't believe I've ever seen a more wonderful sight than the 30lb salmon caught on Loch Druidibeag on the 29th of April, 1952.

The wedding was that of a cousin of my mother, who was marrying a soldier. It was a memorable wedding, and not just because it was the first I ever attended. The bride stayed at our house the night before the wedding, and I remember the sheer sense of fun that went on all night.

My father was a piper and what I remember most, of course, are the great reels and tunes he played while everyone danced. My mother seemed clothed in flour, with clouds of it rising from her arms in the kitchen as she baked and cooked on the griddle over the stove.

God only knows where they got the coloured balls and papier mâché from, but the house was transformed by them, with sprinkles of yellow and blue and red and green festooned everywhere. And we were allowed to eat as much as we could! Someone brought in a trayful of marshmallows and I can still taste the sweetness of the pink and white in my mouth.

The wedding itself was at the church of course, with the groom – who was serving in the Seaforths if I remember correctly – dressed up in his finest. Kilt and hose and *sgian dubh* and a black Glengarry with a tartan trim, I think, and we all stayed ever so quiet at the vows and cheered afterwards as we threw confetti at them as they left the church, making for the hotel and the wedding meal.

This, I now realise, was a bit of a break with convention for most young couples would have their wedding meal in the church hall with the local women providing the food, but I think the soldier must have had a bit of money and would have wanted to make a bit of a splash and have a 'proper' wedding meal at the hotel. I have no idea now what we ate, for all I remember of the hotel are the stairs and the glassed fish, which now seem a bit smaller and more pitiable.

There was a wedding dance too, held in the local village hall, and my memory of that is far less pleasant. I would just have been exhausted, for when I try to recall it now it's one long confused fuzzy recollection with folk dancing and music swirling around and I just so much wanted to get carried home and get into my bed, but the thing seemed endless and I remember putting my head down somewhere and trying to close my eyes, but folk kept interrupting me and asking if I wanted a lemonade or another slice of wedding cake. It may have been the most miserable I've ever been.

And I was on these stairs once before too, at the funeral. I must have been sixteen then, for that's when Iain died, killed by a charging bull in the field between the old school and the river. It was forbidden to go there, of course, which is why we all went there as often as we could or as often as we could get away with it, until the day he charged at Iain and trapped him between the old stone wall and the bog. We never went there again.

And so I stand in the room now, looking down at the splendid sight before me: the Minch red with the reflected light of the sun, setting far to the west in the other direction. I'm facing east here, and can see the distant hills of Skye – the mighty Cuillin hills themselves – shining red and black in the far distance. Perhaps muir fires are burning over Strath way, for I can see some smoke towards the south.

There is no window to the west here, though that has all to do with the hotel's layout rather than tradition. The west window was always to be guarded against: that's where the *Sluagh* – The Host of the Dead – entered. I knew myself of a man who was lifted away by the host on a number of occasions.

He was my immediate neighbour, Fearchar Mac Fhearchair, a big sturdy man almost seven feet tall who was once taken north to Benbecula, once south to Tiree, and once on a long distance journey, to London itself.

'I heard the noise first,' he told me, 'and before I could do anything about it the Host had come in through the small window at the back and lifted me up with them through the skies. Niall Sgròb himself was at the head of The Host, flying with all his might. The first time they brought me down on the rocky skerry on the east coast of Benbecula, where they were kind enough to give me a feed of herring and potatoes. The time they took me to Tiree they tried to tempt me to fling the fairy arrow at a poor woman who was spinning inside her house, but I refused and so was swiftly returned back to my bed. And the last time they lifted me, they took me far south to the big city itself where they showed me all the shining rooftops of the great houses.'

And don't just take my word for it or Fearchar's, because I investigated the matter that year I returned home from university and found nobody who could diminish his evidence. I asked his wife if I could record her about the matter and she finally reluctantly agreed, on three different occasions giving exactly the same testimony as to what had happened.

'The first time,' she said, 'I was out on the hills myself, herding the cattle, when I heard the noise down about the house. So I went down and of course Fearchar was not there, though his pipe lay lit on the table and his meal was still there half-finished. He was three days away that time, and when he came back on the morning of the fourth day he said the *Sluagh* had taken him north across the fords to Benbecula where they'd abandoned him on this remote skerry, though they had been good enough to leave him sufficient food to survive. The best of food it was too – herring and potatoes.'

'And the second time?' I asked.

'Well, the second time, I was in the house myself with him when it happened. Again I heard a noise and when I went down to the bed he'd gone. That time they took him much further away, down to Tiree, but he refused to do their bidding and got safely back home by the following evening. And the third time I was sitting right there with him by the fire when they came and took him away to show him the sights of the great city of London from the air. He saw very wonderful things, as I'm sure he'll tell you himself.'

And indeed he did: he talked of things moving through the air, of things moving fast on iron roads, and of things flying towards the speed of light. Don't we all explain what we have marvellously known? And here I am, finally getting round to it.

Fearchar verified every tale, putting pictures to words and words to pictures. He spoke about the sound the Host made: like a gaggle of geese. He spoke about travelling through the skies: fields and rivers and little villages and big cities moving at a great speed far below. This phrase always appeared in every telling of his travels: 'One minute I was at home; the next, I was somewhere else.'

To be in two locations at once. And I remember as a child staying with an aunt who had a two-storey house, from where you could see as far north as Gerinish. And when night came I slept upstairs near the moon and stars and could hear voices downstairs talking and laughing and singing, and the clink of glasses, and I regretted that there were two different places.

Fearchar himself always travelled by bicycle, and it seemed obvious to me at this point that I too should travel by bike while I was here this time. I scanned the tourist leaflets by my bed and sure enough there was a bicycle hire place by the hotel just up from the pier shop, so the next morning I hired a beautiful red Raleigh which had ten gears. If I had seen such a vision as a child I believe I would have fainted. I leapt on to the bike, and like Fearchar began my journey inland, past the bank and the concrete steps and the old telephone exchange and the shack where the dentist pulled all my back teeth out.

There was the old school, now a ruin, and there too the wooden hut in which Albert, who'd fought in the Boer War and kept pigeons, had lived, and the small knitting factory, now turned into a traveller's bunkhouse. The knitting patterns had become famous all over the world – intricate whorls based on seashells which adorned the jerseys, and then fine wave-like patterns which decorated the mittens and gloves and socks. My own mother had worked there for a while, carding the wool on a brand new machine which Singers had invented, but which then broke and became unworkable. How beautiful her hands were and how delicately she made the scarf she gifted me on my thirteenth birthday. I loved it. It was long and speckled with green and orange dye from the crotal, and when you shook it in the wind you could see the colours rising into the skies.

I stopped at the top of the hill, where there was a signal, and tried to phone Helen, but couldn't get through. It was a clear morning. The local hospital, where my father had died, was about a mile ahead. That too was a bright spring morning: St Patrick's Day.

We'd been out shearing the sheep when he cried out in pain and clutched his hands to his chest, dropping the clippers and allowing the greatest sin: letting a half-shorn sheep run out of the pen. I watched it jumping across the rocks with it's fleece half-hanging from its back. For a crazy moment I wondered whether to rescue the animal or to turn towards my father. By the time I did, he was lying down in the clipped wool, gasping for that empty air. I panicked and tried to pump his chest and raise his arms and rub his face, but it was all over. There were no mobiles then. We were out on the hill on our own. He died in my arms.

The beautiful statue of the Sacred Heart stands outside the hospital, which has now been turned into a nursing home. The brand new hospital lies further to the north. I go over to the image, which is exquisite in its details and in its colours. Christ looks down with compassion, His hands outspread. He wears a beautiful red vestment and the pierced radiant heart lies at the centre of the chest, just to the right of where my father's stopped pumping. I touch his feet with my hands. The stone is warm. On Good Friday you could go up to the altar and kneel and kiss His feet. Throughout the service the priest would slowly unveil the crucifix, bit by bit. When you entered, the Christ, the Saviour of the world, was hidden behind the black cloth, the shame of the universe. Then a shoulder, and another, and a nail-pierced wrist, and another, were revealed before the bells pealed at the end of the day, signalling that Easter and Resurrection day was on the horizon.

And what a glorious day that was – all bells and incense and coloured vestments and the sun dancing in the sky, and the games in the afternoon, with the time of penance over for another whole year – wow, have you really not eaten any sweets at all for seven weeks?! – and the young men whispering about that first drink they would have the next weekend after the long sacrifice of Lent. And how Protestants despised the crucifix with its symbol of the Christ still hanging from the cross.

'Don't you Catholics realise that the cross is now empty? That He is Risen. That it is finished and no more sacrifice is required? Not to mention all your Marian worship!'

Before they too were swept aside by the tsunami of atheism which discarded all our symbols, whether veiled or unveiled, as pernicious.

I cycled inland, past the old school where girls with marvellous names had appeared, like stars on a winter's night: Julianna Johnston, Naoise MacDonald and Diana Richards. Julianna had the best bicycle in the district – a red and green one with twelve gears, which sparkled in the twilight.

We once went on a cycle ride together down on the machair and raced each other across the sand dunes. I tended to be faster on the uphills, but each and every time she would then sweep past me on the downhill, flashing past me like a ferris wheel. After a while we discarded the bikes and went rabbit hunting, using the bike torches as dazzlers to blind the rabbits as they emerged from the sand burrows.

'There's one!' cried Julianna, running across the marram grass, but of course it was still too early in the day to dazzle the rabbits which just hopped merrily across the grass into the next burrow. The torches worked best at night when Uncle Donald and my cousin George would go down after midnight and come back in the early morning with a dozen rabbits in a pouch over their shoulders. I pleaded and pleaded with them, and they finally allowed me to go with them.

It was a cold and clear October night and as we walked down to the machair we all whistled the same tune. We took it in turns to start, and then the others had to guess what the tune was and join in. Donald always began with the pipe march 'Father John MacMillan of Barra' and I can still hear the up-and-down sweetness of that melody in the moonlight.

We caught eighteen rabbits that night. The whistling stopped about a mile from where the rabbits were.

'They'll hear,' said Uncle Donald. 'And also take your boots off now. They can hear that too.'

So we all took our boots off, tied them together with the laces and swung them over our shoulders. Donald went first, leading us crouched to the sandbank.

'We've to work as a team,' he whispered. 'George – you go over to that dune there. I'll go to the one opposite. And you, lad, stay at this one. And don't put that torch on until you hear my shout!'

And the two of them crept away through the moonlight. Clouds came and obscured the light. I lay on my stomach in the dark listening to the silence. Uncle Donald would be over there, to my left. Cousin George over there, to my right.

Everything was still until you started listening. Then you heard everything. My own breath, in and out. My heart beating against the sand. Something was scratching across the grass to my left. A strange bird hooted somewhere. Would Seonaidh the ghost come rattling with his stick across the dunes? Then the shout came.

'*Coineanach!* Rabbit!' And the three torches shone, illuminating the poor creature now frozen in the triple light.

'Stay,' shouted Uncle Donald, and we stayed where we were as he crept towards the blinded rabbit from behind. We kept our lights fixed on the poor rabbit, dazzled by the beams. I could see Uncle Donald now behind the rabbit. He raised his torch and brought it down with a thump on the rabbit's neck, which fell over. Uncle Donald scooped it up and put it into his bag.

'You next!' he shouted, as we all lay back down again in our positions. We kept our eyes scanned on the machair, which was now illuminated by the moon. Then I saw him, some ten feet away from me, peering its little nose out of the rabbit hole. He sniffed the air and retreated back into the burrow, but then came back out again in a few minutes. He sniffed the air again and came forwards slowly, cannily.

I flicked on the torch, shouting '*Coineanach*' as the creature sat five feet away from me, frozen in the torchlight. His teeth chattered. His little feet biting the earth. This was it. The moment had come. I was a man. I crawled forwards and could see the fear in his eyes. He wasn't looking at me. He wasn't looking at anything. Making no plea. Just frozen with terror. I raised my torch and brought it down on the back of his neck as hard as I could with one swift blow. He made no sound as he died, though blood dribbled from his mouth and neck.

We shared the hunt and the spoils that night: six rabbits each. My mother skinned them for me the next morning, showing me how to paunch the animal before removing each leg at the joint with the cleaver, then separating the muscle covering the gut from the skin and pulling that back over the back legs.

'Just like taking your socks off, you see,' she said.

'Then pull the skin forward, like this, and ease out each of the front legs. See? Pull the skin forward then, like this, and if you get hold of that cleaver yourself, you can sever the head.' We removed the tail and the tail glands, then wiped the flesh over with a hot, damp cloth to remove the little traces of fur. We washed it and had a wonderful stew for days on end: rabbit meat, carrots, onions, celery and salt.

Julianna and I tried to kiss, but we weren't very good at it. It felt silly and – frankly – unnecessary. Our two mouths touched and then of course we had no idea what to do, so we just pressed harder but she couldn't really breathe then, and so started coughing and we had to separate. So we just lay back down in the marram grass for a while beside each other, holding hands.

I lay to the right of her, so my left hand was in her right hand, which seemed really awkward because I didn't know whether to put it palm-down into her palm or just to lay it back-hand down on to hers. But she solved the problem by twining her fingers through mine so that my wrist lay against the grass while her fingers lay palm-down on mine. I never knew such slim fingers existed: they were like thin traces of string in my hand. After a while I squeezed her hand, and she squeezed mine back in response. We lay there like that for a while in the silence. Thin clouds moved in fantastic shapes through the sky above.

'It's an elephant,' I said.

'No it's not. It's a giraffe.'

'A panda?'

'No – no no. It's a bear.'

'Do you really think,' she asked, 'that I have the best bicycle on the island?'

'Yes. By far. I wish I had one like that.'

'But it's a girl's bike,' she said. 'With no crossbar.'

I pondered how to respond. I shrugged my shoulders. 'Doesn't matter.'

'Really?'

'Really,' I replied.

We were silent for another while. Then she said. 'Do you really want a shot of it?'

'Yes,' I said.

She sat up on one elbow and looked down on me.

'And promise you won't break it?'

'Promise.'

She shoved me towards the bike and I leapt on to it with glee. Down the machair dunes as fast as Stirling Moss and up the slopes like Robbie Brightwell, with the gears changing through the sandy chicanes and the sparks flying from the back wheel. I freewheeled for a while, raising my feet over the handlebars as the bike travelled down the slope, until it – inevitably – hit the bump and sent me catapulting into the corn. I heard her laughing, and I don't think I ever lived the shame down, though to her eternal credit she never told anyone, but kept it as a dark, unspoken secret between the two of us which kept us apart from then on.

I don't think I even realised it, but I was aiming for the boat. I knew where it was of course – about ten miles to the south, abandoned the last time I'd seen it in the old byre. Would even the byre itself be there now, after all these years? I had lunch by the roadside: sandwiches and some fruit bought from the Coop, and continued to head south. Up south as they said locally, in defiance of cartographic convention where north was always supposed to be 'up' and south 'down'. Or more accurately up sous, because of the loss of the 'th' in Gaelic speech, where the t is always silent so that you say the word '*tha*' meaning 'yes' as 'ha'. The 'th' as an 's' caused great local amusement.

'Help me, I'm sinking,' cried a tourist as he sank into the local bog.

'Oh,' said the local crofter as he walked by, 'What are you sinking about?'

Or the local favourite when all the lads, stuck in the workers' van on a wet day, decided to play I Spy.

'I spy,' said Donald, 'something beginning with S.'

'Socks?' someone suggested. 'Sugar?' 'Shoes?' 'Semmit?' 'Spades?' 'Semolina?'

'No, no, no no...'

Finally they gave up.

'Och, it's so obvious' said Donald. 'So simple – you've been drinking tea out of it all morning. It's the Sermos Flask.'

The wind is in my face, coming warm from the south. I bend down low over the handlebars and cycle steadily, watching the dark whirl of the wheels on the paved road. I weave in and out between the caterpillars crawling ever so slowly across the tarmac. It used to boil up in little bubbles under our bare feet in the summer. The ditch flowers overflow in all their glory – orchids and primroses and spring squills and the beautiful little bog pimpernels, and as I raise my head to go downhill, there's the loch we skated upon one frozen winter, now lipped with marsh marigolds and gilded with lilies. The row our father gave us for skating in such a dangerous place – didn't we know the water-horse lived there who would gobble us up as soon as our foot sank beneath the water?

Old Archie lived with ghosts. He heard hammering during the night and by the following morning the village joiner would be seen out in his yard making a new coffin. He could see things: phantom funerals, portents in the sky, movements in the earth. My brother John and I had a dare: one of us would dress up as a ghost and frighten him one night while the other watched and laughed.

We flung stones on the loch to see who'd be the ghost: loser would be the phantom. My chuckie made fifteen leaps; his fourteen. It all took planning. We took the white sheet out of my mother's kist a week beforehand and hid it away behind our den next to the river. Then on the Saturday night when the whole house was silent and everyone in bed we crept out through the back window and down to the den.

I pinned the white sheet on to him and led him by the hand across the stream and up to old Archie's house where I let him go at the door and then climbed over the wall to peek at the great event.

'Whoo – whoo – whoo,' wailed my brother, but nothing happened.

He grew bolder and walked round the house calling in his best ghost voice.

Finally we heard a noise from inside the house. A candle was lit and I could see the candle moving from old Archie's bedroom towards the little door. My heart was in my mouth. The door opened slowly and there stood Archie in his long white underwear with a nightcap on his head. John had learned his lines.

'Whoooo,' he cried. 'I've come for you! I do not belong to this earth.'

Old Archie listened to him calmly then said,

'I didn't say you did. But then again neither do I. Would you like something to eat?'

John ran as fast as he could, over the garden wall with the white sheet trailing behind him while old Archie stood in the door blessing him in the name of the Trinity.

There's the nurse's little cottage. She would have been there the day I was born, the first person to see me come into the world. I never thanked her either, so I give the bicycle bell a long tinkle. There's the pitch where I used to be Denis Law. On the loch the swans still bend their beautiful necks deep into the water.

I stop by the roadside. This is where the tinker's fair used to be. With their gaunt grey ponies and little carts laden with what seemed to us like the treasures of all the earth: balloons and festoons of coloured ribbons and toys that rattled and moved when you wound them up, and once a talking monkey in a cage who could tell your fortune. You paid him a sixpence and his little shrill voice would sing,

'You'll go far. Far away over land and sea.'

That was to the boys. And to the girls:

'You'll meet a boy. Tall and fair. Maybe even here today.'

The place is now a sheep fank with their little round hard black turds all over the place.

And there on the hilltop is Cnoc nan Each, where the wild horses used to roam. And all round stretch the peat bogs which were once filled with people cutting and lifting the peat, but which today lie empty and silent.

I leave my bike by the road and walk across the bogs to my father's old peat bank which once seemed as large as the promised heavenly mansion. I measure it out. Seven metres by five. I lie down in the shade of the curved stone where I used to lie as a child. Three two one, I found you, you are It! This is where we would have our picnic: bread and cheese, and milk from a corked ale bottle.

Over there stands The Big Stone where the giant lived. If you shouted your name into the hollow, he'd hear and shout it back like an echo. The trick was to shout your name at him and then get away as fast as you could before he called after you. You never made it, even if you ran as fast as Paavo Nurmi himself: no sooner had you called and turned than you would hear his hollow voice calling you back, just by the time you got to the wet dip on the other side of the rock.

They all said that James had managed it once, but no one really believed that.

'James – that cripple!' we'd protest. 'How could he have done it?'

And then they would explain that he hadn't always been crippled and had once been the fastest boy in the whole village until the accident had happened. Then they wouldn't say any more, as if that ended all discussion and argument.

You can see everywhere from here. To the west, right out into the Atlantic as far as America. To the north, up towards Lewis. To the south, down to Barra and to the blue mainland beyond. And to the east, over towards Skye and the high hills of heaven.

I always used to wonder where heaven was. I thought at first that it was up somewhere in the skies, then after my Mum's aunt came home from a visit from Canada I refused to believe that, because I heard her tell my parents about her journey, and how she'd flown first through the clouds and then high above the clouds 'where everything was clear and blue and empty, with no buildings or traffic'. So it couldn't be there, otherwise she'd have seen it and said, for she was an extremely kind and honest woman. She brought us wonderful presents home that year – a ski suit for my brother John and a pair of ice skates for me which I soon ruined by using them on the local quarry slope. It was here after all.

There was the site of the local school which had been demolished in the 1970s. One morning I was the only pupil to arrive there, having walked through the snowstorm. The teacher, Miss MacDonald, lit the peat fire and read me a story. Ivan and the Beech Tree was the name of the story. *Creak, creak, creak said the beech tree* is the only line I remember from the story, except that it was a fantastic story and I remember Ivan got £20,000 out of the trunk of the tree at the end. Or maybe it was £20. What a tragedy we had no trees on our island, though later I found medals stashed between two stones by the river and gave them to my parents. They were from the Peninsular War. At school, Seonaidh and I were the champion fighters: he would sit on my shoulders and between us the two of could shove anyone else off their stance. The game was called *casan-cuinneag*, the legs of the milk churn, with Seonaidh's legs dangling fowards over my shoulders, and my head the milk pail.

It was a Victorian school. By which I mean that it was built in her time, though even in my time we were surrounded by the maps of Empire. How pink the world was, which belonged to us. Look – there's the British Dominion of Canada and all that stretch there, Iain, also belongs to us! Egypt, Sudan, Northern Rhodesia and Southern Rhodesia, India, Burma, Australia and New Zealand. Bets we're the best. And we'd trace the rivers of the world. 'Now, boys and girls, just follow my pointer. There – we'll begin here, between Putumayo and Tabatinga and trace it all the way west. Look – past St Paolo de Olivenwa, then up to Fonteboa, down past Teffe and Manaos and Itacoatiara and Parintins and Santarem and down into and past Almeirim into the mouths of the River Amazon!'

'Sir! Sir! Please – can I hold the pointer? Sir?' And the chosen one would stand there proudly holding the universe at his fingertips. 'Now then, John, point out London to us!' And then a host of hands would go up and each in turn would ask John to locate their own magic name – Rio de Janeiro! Bahia Blanca! Tierra del Fuego! And I asked if I could trace the Nile, and slowly moved north across the Nubian Desert all the way to Cairo and beyond. 'And do you know how long the Nile is?' he asked and we all guessed foolishly. Ten miles. A hundred miles. A million miles. And with a triumph he would tell us, 'Four thousand, one hundred and thirty-two miles,' and of course we would all ask how they knew – did someone go along and measure it, and where did they get a measuring tape that long, and what happened if they made a mistake – would they then have to walk all the way back to the beginning and start all over again? – but the answer was always indistinct and mysterious – 'They have ways.'

My brother and I measured the stream that ran down beside the house. We climbed the small hill to where it began, trickling out of a little hole in the rock and then if you paced it out it was two thousand and twenty-five yards to the sea. The older we got the shorter the distance became. And by the time I left it was only one thousand seven hundred and twenty yards from that first trickle to where the river first met the ocean. Though that too was difficult to define, for it all depended on the tides.

There was a place in Australia we loved. Kalgoorlie and Coolgardie, because they sounded so much like the Gaelic 'cailleach a' mùn air cùl gàrraidh', which means 'an old woman pissing behind a garden wall'. We would forever ask the teacher to tell us about these places so that we could sit there giggling while he innocently went on about them. The ruins of life. Where a previous generation danced in their tackety boots and where an earlier schoolmaster from Birmingham had come and taught cricket and football to my grandparents. He made the foolish mistake of playing the boys against the girls in the first every cricket match, which the boys lost, so the game was never again played.

How locked into time we are, as if nothing happened except that which happened to us. What we heard and saw and felt.

As if these little Iron Age people had never stared at the crescent moon rising over the hill and as if there wasn't a time when there were different maps or no maps or pointers or schools and all the girls slaved from morning till night and all the boys went off to war. There's Easabhal which never had that name until the Vikings came. All those beautiful maps have fallen off the walls, and I can hardly name anything right around here any more. And to know that there will be a time when no one will be left alive who will have known Alasdair or Katell or who will have walked these fields with me. A time when all will be future.

Mrs MacIsaac would always call you in as you walked past and give you black treacly tea and there in the smoky darkness make you eat white buttered bread covered with cats' hairs. I always took a small bite from the edge and stuffed the rest into my pockets and flung it over the wall on my way back home. They have all gone, all these old people with their copper kettles and stoves and patterned plates and dressers, and the tinkers and horses too, and that up-and-down nasal way of speaking, replaced by the marvellous new democracy of digital freedom. Already it is that eternal story that begins once upon a time.

And there's the church. I enter. The holy water font still to the right, and I dip my finger and index finger in and make the sign of the cross. I kneel in the pew at the back and hear the great Latin choral singing from upstairs – *Tantum Ergo Sacramentum, Veneremur cernui* and the old priest bows down at the front, saying *In nomine Patris, et Filii, et Spiritus Sancti. Amen*, and I find myself saying *Introibi et altare Dei. Ad deum qui laetificat juventutem meam*, before the vernacular takes hold, *An ainm an Athar 's a' Mhic 's an Spioraid Naoimh. Amen.*

They breathed in here instead of out, constantly inhaling heaven, rather than expelling earth.

13

FLYING WAS BEAUTIFUL. She'd almost forgotten the rush of relief when the plane finally broke through the clouds on the ascent and then smoothed out, giving you that childish view of the cotton clouds floating below. In the gaps she could see Larkin's England, packed like squares of wheat and then the quick view of the channel before the sharp descent to the Charles de Gaulle. Who was once a soldier and leader but was now an airport. Then later how green the south of France was and how blue the Mediterranean and how red Africa. She'd almost forgotten that first rush of African heat too when you descended from the plane straight into the oven.

She was met by two officers from UNICEF who took her to the hotel where she met up with the other workers and volunteers. She'd almost forgotten that too – that first burst of excitement in meeting new people and the occasional comforting surprise of teaming up once again with an old colleague from some other project years ago.

'Helen!' said Anna. 'Goodness – don't you look wonderful!' Anna from Helsinki who'd worked with her some ten years previously in the Falklands. They embraced. That first night they all had a meal together, rediscovering all the old hopes and fears and anxieties. How one day it would all be unnecessary; how they needed better protection the further they moved inland; the hope that the ongoing peace talks would reach some kind of resolution; and always the concern for the innocents they were there to serve. The women and children.

And little personal stories too. Anna told about her new-born niece who had immediately been taken out by her Saami mother and baptised into the snow.

'A wonderful purification. I now do it myself every morning: go out and immerse myself in the snow. At home, of course. Not much chance of doing that out here!' The sun burned down on them all. And Helen told them all about the old Gaelic proverb which says '*S e deireadh gach cogath sìth*' – 'The end of every war is peace. And since that's always the case, it makes you wonder why they bother with it in the first place!'

Five thousand had already died that year in the war which had come to some sort of end with an uneasy ceasefire three months previously. Anna and Helen and Irene and Johan and Vincent were all to work together up in the north, helping out the nuns and doctors at the St Vincent de Paul Hospital who were treating the burn victims.

The journey to the hospital was a long, forty-eight-hour ride in a Land Rover across rough tracks. They all initially felt sick from the inoculation jabs they'd received but by the morning of the second day all were in good spirits. How unique the desert environment really was: once you left the gorgeous beaches near Mogadishu and moved north you realised very quickly how utterly dependent on the environment everyone was. The power of water, of green things, those little oases in the desert which sustained life and gave hope and raised strength. Like little winter cèilidhs which sustained you all the way through till springtime.

And the sweetness of fruit under the burning sun. How the mangoes seemed to liquify your entire body, and then that constant need for water as you moved further and further north. How a slice of orange from the cold bag in the back of the Land Rover or a segment of pineapple sustained you forever. And then how suddenly darkness came and how astonishingly cold it was so quickly after the long burning day. Stars would emerge and lights would twinkle in the dark blue sky and you remembered with anguish how gorgeous the world was and how fantastic it was to be alive, and what it felt like to say 'Look – there's Venus!' and then watch as your friend Anna gazed up and tried to see exactly what you were seeing.

The hospital itself was a simple old building which had managed to survive the ravages of war, though not without damage. It was run by locals with some expatriate specialist help and dealt as best it could with illnesses as well as with conflict-related injuries. They treated cholera on a weekly basis when doctors came from Mogadishu itself, and on a daily basis with everything from malnutrition to limb loss. Somehow, music had veined itself into the running of the hospital, and a number of former patients would sit in any shaded corner playing little instruments which literally oxygenated the air. You could almost see patients improve every time they passed Abuukar playing his *oud* or old Mahad beating his little drum.

You never forget how to heal. You listen, and love with your eyes and then take them into the antiseptic room and clean the wounds. Little licks with the pinhead brush, and the dab of liquid antiseptic and the plaster which always reassures the patient that someone cares, that another human being is concerned and will do her best so that you might possibly live. Helen always knew that the greatest care was in the actual physical touch, as you gave the anti-cholera drug or cleaned the shrapnel wound or helped the woman as she gave birth. Valuable as all her environmental work was, this was really where her heart lay: in this care work, learned over a lifetime of experience. It was her mother in the orchard, her Dad with his little red melodeon. It was Bella Campbell that time she came visiting and treated seven-year-old Helen for a badly grazed knee. Bella lifted her up and carried her down to the river where she washed the wound in the cold running water and then dabbed the area with *buadhalan buidhe* – ragwort – gathered from the side of the stream.

Bella was full of wondrous natural cures – how you

ANGUS PETER CAMPBELL

should rub a *seilcheag* – a slug – on a cold blister to cure it, and chew *cairt shleamhna* – tormentil – for a sore lip. For a simple headache Bella would boil the leaves of *Lus nan Laogh* – Buckbean – and make you drink that water first thing in the morning. She even had a cure for constipation, which was to take fresh sea tangle, cut it in pieces and give to the patient to chew and swallow. She knew of course – but didn't practice – some of the more outlandish methods, though she delighted in telling young Helen about them. For stomach ache, for example, if a patient was in real desperation you could put a rope round his feet and hang him by the heels from the rafters.

'But you must repeat it at reasonable intervals,' she would then say, 'for that will undo the knot in his guts.' And on several occasions she showed Helen and her Mum how to make an emergency bandage. 'You skin an eel in long strips and wrap it round the strain or sprain as a bandage with the fat side in. The eel fat soothes, and the skin, being elastic, will not bind too tightly. Best,' she always added, 'if you get the patient to stand for an hour or so in the stream beforehand, for the cold will ease the swelling.' Helen knew full well that the local people here would also have their wonderful ancient cures, though she was never given the time to find out.

There was no mobile signal from the hospital except that once every few weeks one of the younger local doctors from Mogadishu would come north with medicines and take with him a sort of home made satellite dish which gave a signal for a while on his own phone. It was from that contraption that Helen managed to contact me on that final May evening. Along with all the others, Helen had no chance as soon as the line went dead. It had all, I suppose, just been a matter of time. The political or religious explanations just made it all the more senseless. All of them were gunned down in a matter of minutes for no reason except the old reason: that they were symbols of the enemy.

I heard the initial news by mobile right there in heaven, at the peat bog. I just listened to the quiet voice of the man from the Foreign Office who had been delegated the job of phoning me. He asked me if I wanted the body brought home and I said I didn't know. He expressed his sorrow and said that I could phone him back any time day or night when I'd had time to deal with the news. He said that some had already chosen for their loved ones to be buried there, in the nunnery's small cemetery. I thanked him and switched the phone off.

I lay down in the bog in the dry curve between the two rocks where sheep sheltered in the winter, staring up into the cloudless sky broken only by the white vapour of a jet moving silently to the north-west. Grief holds no boundaries. The underground streams ran beneath my back: they eventually emerged about a mile west, where the white water cascaded over the cliffs. Barriers are useless. The tears flowed down my cheeks for all the loveliness that was extinguished. Everything was finished, even though a butterfly – the common blue – suddenly hovered beside me like a child, before vanishing.

None of this was supposed to have happened. The plan really had been to find the old boat and maybe restore it and sail it back down to Mull sometime with Helen. Except I hadn't told her. Had kept it secret, even from myself. The secrecy broke me. This great big bloody secrecy, as if life was a mystery to be hidden rather than a wonder and a revelation. I didn't know the woman: didn't know her at all, really. She was still a dream when it came down to it. A stranger who had crossed my path, and I a stranger who had crossed hers: two mature people who had shared a few things and had excluded nearly all that really mattered.

Maybe it had just been a matter of time: had we had more time, what we would or could have achieved, together. Had we actually met that first time round, how different things might have been. The world we would have painted. Had we really loved each other, we would never have separated. I didn't even have her picture except on my phone. I switched it back on, but the power had gone.

I'd had enough of ashes. I asked her. Would she prefer to

be buried in Africa or in Mull? She hesitated and replied that love was all, and that she should be buried in the place she loved. I too then hesitated. Does love have a geography? An environment. I looked around me, at this place I loved. I had never loved anything or anyone more than I loved this place. Not Margherita or Marion or Helen or Juliana or anyone else in the whole world, except this mysterious place which had framed my childhood.

'I shall bury you here,' I said, 'alongside myself and all that I have carried.'

Life was all. Was everything. I cycled down through my home village and found a roadside phone box which still worked and phoned the man at the Foreign Office and told him that Helen should be brought home. He promised it would be done, though of course it would take a few days, but the RAF had already been informed about others and things were being put into place.

I asked her whether I too should return but she told me to stay. Or at least the wind or the waves or the tide or the rocks did, for it began to rain and with it the whole island became a place of mist and loss. Stay, she said. But go back to the hotel first. Rest. Think and pray about me. Make up a votive offering if need be, if it helps. Shout if needs be. Or whisper. It may be that the voice is not in the wind or in the earthquake or in the fire but in the stillness.

So I cycled back to the hotel through the pouring rain. Past the pitch where I later became Jimmy Greaves. The hotel bath was old-fashioned and the water took ages to run to heat through the pipes, but eventually bubbled through. I made a boat out of the soap and stuck a toothpick in it for a mast and sailed it beneath the bridge of my legs. No matter which way I pushed, it always drifted upwards towards my chest where it would come to rest. I called it *An Leumadair Gorm* – the Blue Dolphin – and sailed it backwards and forwards in the great tide of the bath until it melted into soft lather. I would go the following morning.

It rained all night. One of those wild early summer storms which come so suddenly and with such ferocity, and then dissipate equally as quickly, leaving no lasting damage. All sound and fury signifying nothing. In the morning, everything shone bright and wet after the long night's rain. This was it.

I cycled west again, past all of yesterday's memories, towards the summer where Big Roderick and I had built the boat. I arrived at the place where Donald ought to have come from Woodstock, but didn't, and looked towards where we would have been, on the slight incline of the hill just above the bay. I so much wanted Alasdair and Kate to be there waiting, not for me but for him.

On the left hand side of the track was the roadside shrine to the Virgin. As was the custom, I came off my bicycle and made the sign of the cross as I passed the shrine. I then remounted and slowly ascended the hill which would finally take me down into the bay. I paused at the top for a moment and then freewheeled it to the bottom, the wind accelerating into my face. I parked the bike by the cattle grid which signalled the start of the village and walked over the small hill which led to the bay where we'd launched *The Blue Dolphin* that other summer's day.

It is empty and quiet. Nothing can be seen or heard except for the oystercatchers darting about the edge of the sand. How blue the sea is, and how clean. Cerulean. You feel it could rinse the world. It is the morning of the seventh day.

I scramble over the rocks to where she'd been anchored. The tide is out and the rocks are covered in seaweed. I stumble on something, and there it is: the old rope still there, tied to the peaked rock. I go down on my knees and feel the rope, which is still strong and thick. I put one hand in front of the other and trace its path out beyond the rocks towards the sand. Halfway into the sand the rope changes and becomes a chain. My heart leaps. Hah! The anchor chain. So – after all these years, the anchor chain is still here, firm in the sand. I keep my hand on the link-chain until it begins to disappear into the sand. I pull and it moves a fraction, but that's it: I know from experience that the anchor itself is buried deep in the sand now, covered by almost half a century's silt. Not even one of Fearchar's giants could move it now. A digger or a JCB might, but the sacrilege would destroy all of history.

I go on my knees in the sand and kiss the anchor chain. I can see the ruins of Alasdair and Katell's old cottage in the distance, halfway up the hill. I can see the byre too where we'd left the boat all these years ago. I need to walk there: the bicycle needs to be abandoned. Gingerly across the cattle grid, sidestepping, then down past the old stone wall and up by the stream. An old cartwheel lies abandoned there. Grass has grown on the walls of the old mill.

The house itself is in not too bad a shape, though totally uninhabited for years. There are no doors or windows, though somehow the roof is still on and the hearth and parts of the internal walls can still be seen. That's where Katell baked the scones, and that's where she served out the pastries and the *galletes* and over there is where they slept, beneath the south facing window. And this is where the fire was, where all the great stories were told and of course that's where the table would have been where the cheese was sliced and the pickle served and the ham placed on the best plates.

I move out towards the byre, which seems much more secure that the house itself. The roof is still on and the old stone wall is all intact and the single small window at the north end still whole and unbroken. The door is still also there and barred across with a wooden stanchion as it always was by Alasdair. It is as if he fixed it up yesterday and went for a wee holiday. It's jammed tight and I can't move it and I don't want to break it so I go to the tiny window to see if I can peer through. It is all dusty and murky and I can't see a thing though the old single pane of glass. I stand back. Maybe like that other crippled man I need to get up on to the roof and be lowered through a hole.

I go back to the door and try again. Then I notice that it is not jammed at all: it is merely that I was pushing in the wrong direction. How Alasdair would have laughed, and how Big Roderick would have scoffed.

'You with all your Education! Don't you know the difference between push and pull? If you can't pull, *a' bhalaich*, then *slaod*!'

And I did *slaod*, and the batten rose and the door hinge creaked and opened before me.

I entered, and there she was still secure in all her splendour: *An Leumadair Gorm, The Blue Dolphin*, sitting on her battens like a battleship waiting to be launched, like a bird waiting to take off. She rather reminded me of the way the heron stands on a rock waiting for that unknown moment when she suddenly decides to fly with her wings extended and expanded in that wonderful curve.

With the door open there was now sufficient light to see the original boat in all her beauty. She really was elegantly crafted, and age and time had only added to the grace with which she'd been made. I felt her in the half-light with my hands: the clinchers and gaffs and braces and thole-pins and all the other little sensuous parts I'd almost completely forgotten about, and which had been so lovingly handled and finished and polished by Alasdair himself. Was this the one who would not fade?

I placed my hand at the *ceann-ùrlair* – the head – and stroked the boat, touching the garb and the rebat and the apron and the breast-hook and the rubbing-piece and oh I could go on forever, through the pintle and the hanks and the cleats right down to the yoke and the pin and the sheafswallow. Dust covered my hands as I brushed along the wood. A solid old drum was in the corner and I rolled it over, so that I could stand on it and climb into the boat. I sat in the stern with my hand on the tiller and steered her westwards down through the narrow channel between the reefs, out towards the herring banks which lie just west of Fiudaidh. As I sailed her, Alasdair stood in the bow shouting and pointing excitedly out west, where the dolphins leapt and danced in their hundreds. We had a grand catch that day: five crans of herring, and afterwards Katell fried them in oatmeal and butter, and *Ruairidh Mòr* – Big Roderick – ate so many of them that he nodded off for a while after tea, muttering little indistinguishable things to himself. Ruairidh Mòr, who would now find this world he had prophesied so alien.

And the pity that she was here hidden, behind the doors of an old barn. Like some kind of dirty secret. A great thing discarded when she could be a swan in the water, sailing in the Minch, across the Atlantic, through the Panama Canal. Round Cape Horn and the Cape of Good Hope and Cape Cod. Catching lobsters and crabs, herring and mackerel, dolphins and whales and sharks. Her prow cutting the waves, her sails fluttering in the breeze, blowing in the wind. The now so well seasoned wood flying through the water.

Big Roderick loved whistling. Sailing homeward to Mingulay. Call all hands to man the capstan, see the cable run down clear, heave away and with a will boys, for old England we will steer, and we'll sing in joyful chorus in the watches of the night and we'll sight the shores of England when the grey dawn brings the light, rolling home, rolling home, rolling home, across the sea, rolling home to dear old England, rolling home, dear land to thee. Farewell and adieu unto you Spanish ladies as we hunt the bonny shoals o' herrin'.

I love you. *'S toigh leam thu. Tha gaol agam ort. Tha gradh agam ort.* I love you. Love I you. Love have I on you. Love have I on you. And how Donald would have loved her too. Carrying summer visitors over to Barra.

For some reason Abramovitch and his yachts came to mind. I came out of the byre into the sunlight in the full knowledge that what I had greatly loved had diminished every other thing worthy of affection. The boat was not mine, really, so I closed the byre door behind me and walked down the single-track road towards the bike which I'd left by the cattle grid.

A young boy and girl – they would have been no more than ten or eleven – cycled towards me and gave me a friendly wave as they rode by. I looked back over my shoulder at them as they disappeared down the hill, laughing and whooping.

I hope they will kiss like I did, and that it will last forever, like a clear, spoken secret which will bind them together like a spider's glue.

14

HELEN WAS LAID to rest in the place that she loved. The place is under the shelter of Càrn Mòr, and as you go there to remember, gives you a wonderful view over Loch a' Tuath towards Fladda and Lunga, Gometra and Ulva. I too came back here, because the place that I loved was no more, if it had ever been.

I rented a little cottage at the other end of the island, down near Loch Buidhe. It is perfectly placed – sheltered by Beinn Buidhe on one side and by Beinn na Croise on the other, with shore-side access to the loch itself, where I keep a little engine boat.

Helen's will asked for her house to be sold and the monies given to Oxfam and the profits from any of the household contents to be given to the local branch of the RNLI. She asked that I would deal with any personal items as I saw fit. I gave all the clothes to the Salvation Army and offered all her books to the local library. I saved her violin, and the lovely old writing desk with all the materials that were on it for my own little cottage.

I had that horrible day of burning things: watching smoke rise and throwing all the useless little left over things that nobody wanted into the flames. Who was I to decide what was useless? But what was I to do – hand the job over to some stranger, as if that made it any better? Love has to burn as well as glow.

I remembered my mother's funeral and how in those days we did it ourselves. The local villagers dug the grave and when it came time for the burial it wasn't handed over to any professional undertaker. We all lowered the coffin into the sand, and then took it in turns to fill in the grave. There was no final denial that it had really happened: as you flung down the sand with your shovel and then slammed the earth on top to bed it all in, you knew the job was all done. From beginning to end, from head to foot, dust to dust. Here, I had to fight for that right, as the official undertakers tried to shoo us all away for tea and soup and scones while they finished the job.

Some things could not be burned. My father used to say that every crust of bread we flung into the fire would return to us as cinder in the afterlife, and that to tear a page out of a book was a greater sin than stealing. All my life I've had a horror about the burning of books, and I can imagine no greater tragedy than to see print going up in flames. I've done it of course and even taken delight in screwing up old tabloid papers and lighting the fire, but still regretted it. Even the things I didn't like. I once burnt a Reader's Digest and I can still see the words turning to black cinder before going grey and white and out of sight.

I mind once being in an old woman's house in Uist as she was trying to light her fire. The peat was damp, and of course there were no firelighters, and just a couple of poor looking sticks, so she went down to the closet and came back with this old book and began tearing leaves from it, scrunching them up and putting them in the bottom of the grate. She lit them and before long had enough of a fire going to put the kettle on the hob. The book was an ancient copy of Dwelly's dictionary. 'Donald used to look at it now and again,' she said. 'Now it's no use to anyone. And of course I can't read.'

I'm afraid I was too young at the time to challenge her or to rescue the book. And of course she was right – of what use is a book to someone who can't read? Far better for it to be used to light the fire, to give heat and help in making a cup of tea.

And who was I to tell any of my elders what to do with their own property?

I mind the famous MacMhuirich manuscripts which contained all the great and ancient lore of the MacMhuirich poets of South Uist: they say that the last remnants of these writings dried up and were finally used by a peasant descendent to tie his boots together. And rightly so: for who could walk the boggy moors with flapping boots when a perfectly reasonable set of shoelaces could made out of rolled vellum?

Helen left notes and letters and a lifelong diary which I refused to burn. She'd left no specific instructions about them, and of course were not for sale for charitable or any other purposes. They were not 'valuable' enough to be given to any university – for who cares about the writings of an unknown individual who has not claimed fame in the columns of the newspapers or in the critical journals of academia? For the writings of the great and the good, of course, are far more important than the scrawls and scribbles of the untutored amateurs. Or at least were, until the great world wide web came along giving us all a global platform from which to spout our thoughts, ideas, notions and prejudices. For now everyone is king of the castle with equal claim to be heard, or ignored. More people now read my twitterings on twitter than ever read MacMhuirich.

I had a computer for a while, but have now gotten rid of it because it came to possess me. My every moment from dawn till dusk was somehow taken with it, trawling all the news engines of the world for the latest developments, but then being constantly sidetracked by fantastic articles about the Coral Oceans and the Hadron Collider and the decline of the pheasant peacock in Norway and the intricate workings of the steam engines in the old Caledonian trains, and – look – there's that exquisite goal that Messi scored against Milan right now, once again, on YouTube.

So one day I logged off, and because I am a man of ritual carried the computer down into the boat, started the engine and headed off towards the Garvellachs where I dumped it into the deepest part of the ocean west of Eileach an Naoimh. Sorry about the pollution.

I'd been there before, years and years ago, the summer I'd worked on the lobster boat out of Oban. We would sail out late on the Sunday night and spend the week down about the Garvellachs, returning on the Thursday night for the fishmarket. There was just the boat owner and I – a two-man crew.

We took it in turns to steer the boat, though when it came to the lobster grounds he tended to take the wheel while I released the creels into the water. We had about two hundred creels altogether which we moved around from place to place, never setting more than about ten of them in any one place at any one time.

The best places were always just about a mile or so offshore where the skerries tended to deepen and which gave a wonderful undersea craggy environment to the lobsters. There our creels would lie, maybe for about twenty-four hours, baited with fish-heads, and when we returned to gather them each of them would invariably be filled with two or three fine looking lobsters.

Gathering them in was of course quite a tricky job. Often there was a swell, and you had to be really careful not to get the incoming rope tangled in the winch. Though some small boats, even then, had a powered winch, we still just had a hand-pumped one so while the skipper kept the boat bobbing in just the right place I winched and simultaneously lifted the lobsters out of each creel as they ascended.

Often, of course, we got more than we bargained for – all kinds of weird and wonderful things would come out of the sea trapped within the creel, but they were all then pitched over the other side. The only market was for lobster and all other species were useless.

The worst time was when the creels were coming in fast – so fast that you didn't really have time to see what was actually in the creel. You turned the winch handle and, blind as it were, with your back to the incoming creel stuck your hand inside the hole and lifted out the lobster, making sure its claws didn't sink into your wrist. Then with one swift move you wrapped the claws round tight with a thick elastic band and flung the live lobster into the water barrel where you kept them until you came ashore on the Thursday.

But as I put my hand into the creel something bit and as I turned to look this ugly looking fish – I discovered afterwards it was called a catfish – had bitten into my finger. I stepped back, slipped and tumbled overboard.

I remember the faint shadow of the side of the boat appearing above me through the sea and I also remember thinking, I shall now float down to the bottom of the ocean, where I shall die. I thought that because I was in an utterly foreign environment.

I couldn't swim at the time, and had never actually been in the water until that point. Oh, I'd paddled about at the edge of the ocean and all that, but that was actually the first time that I had ever put my whole head and body under the water. Maybe I should add that I had not even done that in the bath, for I am old enough to have been brought up in a house which had no electricity or running water and our weekly bath consisted of a family dip into the zinc tub in front of the peat fire on a Saturday night. We washed our heads first and then sat in the bath up to our necks. It never entered our minds to sink into the whole water with our whole bodies.

So there I was in sinking into the Atlantic in that way for the first time. And then I surfaced and gasped for breath and sank again. My heavy sea boots dragged me down and I knew for certain that this was it. Had I read or heard somewhere that you sink and rise three times, and that was it? Or was that an old wives' tale too? And I surfaced and there was the skipper at the side of the boat holding out the boat hook towards me. I lunged and miraculously grabbed it, and he hauled me aboard. We lost the creels, but who cares?

I think now of the insanity of it all. How we take the greatest risks in innocence, and how we die through ignorance. I think part of it was purely practical – that sea-going communities felt it was pointless to learn to swim because if you fell overboard far out in the Atlantic, it was best to drown quickly rather than prolong the agony. But a good part of it too was mythological: that to dip with the devil was to invite him in. Better to leave him to his deadly devices. However, what this ultimately meant, of course, was defeat. The sea was too powerful. The wind was too strong. The rain was too heavy. The port was too far away. Power lay elsewhere, far away – over the headland, towards the mainland somewhere. For what can I do when the storm comes, or the catfish bites, or the words run out?

Helen's notes and letters and diaries lay there for a long time. Then they gave me voice. I remember the day I finally persuaded myself to look at them, to enter that dead territory where I imagined they lay, only to discover that this was not a cobwebbed crypt but a living gift.

It was a Saturday morning – one of those pleasurable autumn mornings just after the mist has risen off the loch and the whole world is bathed in a soft glow. The coffee bubbled in the pot and once I'd poured it into the mug I made for the small glass porch I'd built at the front of the house. It gathers the sun in the early morning, and it was such a morning. The door to the small study where her papers lay was open and a shaft of light was pouring in through the window directly on to her diaries. I went over and handled them again and took them with me out into the porch.

Do you need permission to enter private territory? And the sun continued to shine. The coffee tasted perfect. What a beautiful rounded hand she had with the Cs and the Fs and the Ls curved and smoothed. Later they turned into a slightly finer script, but kept the open quality which made them so attractive throughout.

Here was her life, or at least those little segments which she'd happened to jot down: the time she climbed Ben Nevis, the time she holidayed with her mother in the Seychelles, the day the dog died. I only glanced for a couple of minutes, not really reading anything, and understood my sin: reducing things to the recorded. Our voice really lay in the gaps. What courage love requires. In the end it is nothing but courage.

And I think that's when it dawned on me that talking wasn't an extra to be done when all other options had run out, but was life itself. For when all doing ceased, then nothing was left but being. We hadn't shared enough. Blethered enough. Spoken, laughed, cried, hoped, planned. We hadn't spent purely nonsensical hours telling jokes or playing cards or making love or singing old hymns or cutting each other's toenails bellowing, 'Oooof – what a smell!' Natasha was right: silence was the real crime against humanity.

When she wrote she used an old-fashioned ink pen. I finished my coffee and went to her desk and sat down. Her fiddle was resting on its stand by the wall next to the bureau. The unlined foolscap paper she used still lay on the left hand side of the desk. The ink well was dry so I rummaged in the drawers and found three unopened ink refills in the bottom drawer – one marked 'Red Ink', one marked 'Black Ink' and one marked 'Green Ink'. I wondered whether she used one for her notes, one for her letters and one for her diaries but didn't wish to check: that belonged to the gaps. I opened the ink bottle marked green and poured the contents into the inkwell on the desktop.

The pen too was without a nib, but in the other drawer I found the case marked 'Nibs'. I'd forgotten the variety of nibs that were available, and how beautiful they all were in their individual ways. I spent an hour or so trying them all out: the long thin elongated one which gives you a spiral-like hand, the shorter more stubby one which gives you the rounded cursive, and all the ones in between which alter your writing – or at least your writing style – depending on which way you hold them.

I was back at school with the dip pen. The school master carefully pouring the black ink into all our little wells. It smelt tarry. Then standing there teaching us how to hold the dip pen – the thumb on the inside wood firmly but not too firmly about a quarter of an inch above the nib, and the forefinger and the index finger balancing the other side. A slight dip of the nib into the ink, for too much would clog it all up and too little would be of no use, and then lifting it gently without dripping over the paper.

First thing were the vowels – and we all invariably made the same mistake, scratching our way downwards, then stopping, and connecting the other side to the downward slope. 'No no no no,' he would say, 'the aim is to try and make it all the way round with just the one stroke.'

And he would lean over us, his smoky and sometimes whisky breath close to our ears, cupping his hand over ours. 'Like this – see. Down and round and up. Down and round and up. Down and round and up.' And eventually most of us got it – dipping the nib, shaking the pen, and away we went a b c d e f g h i j k l m n o p q r s t u v w x y z.

I'd forgotten none of it. I cased in the nib onto to the pen, dipped it in the green ink, gave it a little shake, and began writing. No – that's a lie. You never just begin writing. It's just like these pole-vaulters who spend forever rocking backwards and forwards, backwards and forwards, with the pole in their hands looking up and down before they launch themelves into the run which will take them heavenwards.

I think I doodled for a while, and likely went through the alphabet practising my lettering: the vowels first, as taught in that other century by Mr MacPhie, and then the consonants. A E I O U, and then B C D F G H J K L M N P Q R S T V W X Y Z. How different they looked when small or big. Lower and upper case they called it, as in the Indian castes.

Amo, I wrote. Then Amas, Amat, Amamus, Amatis, Amant. Ablative, I wrote, enjoying the sound of that lovely word on my lips. ABLATIVE. Dative, I then wrote. And made a block on the paper and wrote:

Nominative
Vocative

Accusative
Genitive
Dative
Ablative

Latin and Gaelic. The Latin Mass and the Vernacular. Beside Nominative write Porta. Dorus. Door. Then make the block:

Nom:	Porta.	Dorus.	Door.
Voc:	Porta.	A' Dhoruis!	O Door!
Acc:	Portam.	Dorus.	Door.
Gen:	Portae.	Doruis.	Of the Door.
Dat:	Portae.	An, 'n dorus.	To the Door.
Abl:	Porta.	Doruis.	By/With/From the Door.

That was no story. So I wrote 'The door was closed. The man walked to the door. 'O door,' he said, 'Open'. But the door did not open. He then saw the door's handle. The handle of the door. He bent over to the door, inspected it and walked away from the door.' Not much of a story really, but at least it did take in all the declensions.

I tried it in Gaelic.

'*Bha an dorus dùinte. Choisich an duine chun an doruis. 'A' Dhoruis,' thuirt e. 'Fosgail'. Ach cha do dh'fhosgail an dorus. Chrom e null chun an doruis, choimhead e air agus choisich e air falbh on dorus.*'

It worked more or less the same whichever way you tried it.

What if the door was not closed though? I started again. 'The door was open.' No – that wasn't right either. Maybe it was neither open nor closed – half-open or half-closed, as it were? Now then how would I say that? 'The door was neither open nor shut'? 'The door was half-open'? 'The door was half-closed'? Did they all mean different things? Of course they did. 'The door was neither open nor shut' left things – well, undecided. It left all the possibilities open. Or shut. 'The door was half-open' suggested that it had been closed and had just been opened. Or maybe that it had been open and had just been half-closed. Or maybe just it had been left that way for a long time. Perhaps even for a long long time. Maybe it was a door half off its hinges which could neither open nor shut properly. Maybe it was a gate out in the yard which, being left open, was a huge danger: perhaps a bull might escape through it. Maybe it had been left half-open by a thief, fleeing in the night. By a murderer in a panic, by a man in a hurry.

I wondered about the door. And also about the man. Was the door more important than the man, or the man more important than the door? Had he just noticed the closed/open/half-open/half-shut door and wondered what lay behind it? Was he just making for the bedroom, to find the door closed in front of him? Was he just walking past when a woman came to the door and opened the door for him? And as for the Vocative! Who on earth would address a door? 'O door, where is thy sting?' 'O door, O door, wherefore art thou.' 'Door – open!' Sesame.

'It was a long hot summer,' I wrote. That's it. That was the idea. The idea was everything. That's what it was: a really hot long summer. But I didn't – really – need the really, and for some reason 'long hot summer' sounded better than 'hot long summer'. Maybe simply because it was longer than it was hotter: it was hot in parts, but it felt long. Long in the sense that I've never forgotten it. So. It was a long hot summer.

It was a long hot summer. It was the summer which meant everything to me for the rest of my life. The summer by which I measured hope, success, regret, failure. I picked up a book from Helen's desk. 'To Janet' it said on the inside cover. 'With best wishes. From Robert, Alex and Chris. Xmas 1948.' I turned to the first story. It read: 'Christopholus is eight. He is the only man in the family, as his father sailed away to America to make money, and never came back.'

What a fantastic start to a story, I thought. It's clear, decisive and immediately sets the pace. It was a long hot summer. I looked at other openings. A king once had twelve most beautiful daughters. A poor woodcutter lived with his wife and three daughters in a little cottage on the edge of a lonely forest. The King of the East had a beautiful garden, and in the garden grew a tree that bore golden apples. In the beginning God created the heavens and the Earth. There was once a King's son, who had a sweetheart, and loved her much. Once upon a time there was a dear little girl who was liked by everyone who met her, but especially by her grandmother, who would have given her anything. 1801 – I have just returned from a visit to my landlord – the solitary neighbour that I shall be troubled with. He lay flat on the brown, pine-needled floor of the forest, his chin on his folded arms, and high overhead the wind blew in the tops of the pine trees. Call me Ishmael. Alexei Fyodorovich Karamazov was the third son of a landowner from our district, Fyodor Pavlovich Karamazov, well known in his own day (and still remembered among us) because of his dark and tragic death, which happened exactly thirteen years ago and which I shall speak of in its proper place. There is a lovely road that runs from Ixopo into the hills.

Now isn't that fantastic stuff? A stage for the play. A frame for the picture. Though of course the play and the picture came first. Island. Country. World. Universe. Past. Future. None of it matters but the imagination.

What I really want to do is to write about Helen, since I dreamed about her all my life and when I came to know her I never came to know her at all. And these notes and letters and diaries, even if I were to read them, would tell me so little. And I want to write about Margherita, for I recall her standing that evening on top of the stone wall and shouting to me across the abandoned sheep fank to my left, and the mad romance we had and the glory of it all. And I want to include the wife I had, Maid Marion. And the backdrop to all that must be that summer: that long hot summer we spent building the boat. There is a lovely road.

So I began. It was a long hot summer. And then it needed a pause. A colon. It was a long hot summer: one of those which stays in the memory for ever. It was universal – it belonged to everyone. Like this house which I rent and which is not mine but which I inhabit. Who knows who was in it before me, and who knows either who'll be in it after? And that's where the idea of the violin came in: something lost, and then found, but only to discover that it belonged to no one in the first place. And the boat: could that beautiful boat be reborn?

I remembered John Gordon of Cluny, who owned everything and ended up in a vault beneath Lothian Road in Edinburgh. And the rest was all imagination: pure, unadulterated truth. There was a gorgeous girl I saw on the ferryboat, and we hunted rabbits, and I gave preposterous lectures, and I watched toy yachts race on a Parisian lake, and jazz played through the morning air, and old men played cribbage, and old women played whist and Lachlan went out fishing, and I almost drowned. And she walked down Byres Road and saw that life-changing advert in the newsagent's window, and cycled off round the bollards across the pier, and played the fiddle, and worked in Madagascar and Peru and elsewhere, and told me the Norse version of Chicken Licken, and all about Tikki Tikki Tembo-no Sa Rembo-chari Bari Ruchi-pip Peri Pembo, and finally held my hand on a still summer's day at a railway station.

I strove so hard too to give her voice, and failed. How I loved, she said. And do you remember that time I abseiled down the gorge, and the time I was chased through the New Hampshire woods by a bear, and the time I cried when I heard Maria Callas sing out in the open air in Athens? I was small, and had freckles like the poppies of the machair and always gashed my knees when playing and they always called me a tomboy, and my favourite thing was to guddle for fish in the little streams down by the Aros Burn on a summer's eve. And on Saturdays we would go up to Tobermory and spend the morning looking in the shop windows and sampling the dainties which tasted so sweet. And do you remember that time my friend Lyn and I stood outside the cake shop window and right at that moment the cake stand collapsed and old Ernie came running out of the shop shouting at us that we'd hit the window and caused the cake to fall, which we hadn't? And the time I sat on the pavement and Mrs MacPherson stopped and said to me 'Don't sit there or you'll get dysentry!' And at first it was an all-girls school, but that changed at the end of my first year when it went comprehensive, and did I ever tell you about the day Mr Guthrie fell on top of the Bunsen burners and almost burnt himself – and the school – to ashes?

I loved him. With all the sweetness of young love. He had a car and on Friday and Saturday nights we would go for runs right across the island. Sometimes we would stop at secluded lay-bys, just to listen to some music and kiss. Luxemburg was all the rage then, because you could get a signal almost anywhere. Even deep in the forest where we sometimes drove when the gates were left open. And then of course we split up over something so trivial that I still remember it: his insistence that I should wear my hair down all the time, while I preferred to tie it up.

We used to go to the Highland Games. Not because it meant anything to us culturally or because we competed or anything, but because it was such fun. Such daft, pointless, wonderful fun. We went as a crowd of course, because these things are no fun on your own. Always girls too – girls together. We would spend the previous night at one of our houses, dressing up and putting lipstick on and trying out all the make-up we had and forever listening to music. 'No – he won't be there,' one of us would say and of course all the others would swear by God that of course he would be for we'd heard him say so the day before. And of course he would be, all dress and swagger, running across the field like a gazelle at the start of the hill race. Some of the fairground things would be there, of course, which were such fun – the helter-skelter and the wheel and, once, a machine which took four of us at a time then fired us all straight up into the air at a huge rate of knots, where we paused for some second before being catapulted down again. The joy of course was having your stomach on the ground as you were high up in the air, and then the opposite: leaving your tummy hanging high as you plummeted screaming to earth. And the day always ended up the same: waltzing along to the village hall for the dance where all the girls danced together until the boys finally arrived, high as kites, after the pub had closed. As soon as they arrived the eightsomes and the strip-the-willows would begin in earnest, and what I remember from then on is merely the sound: swish and hooch and swing. I would always lie awake that night, the sound of pipe music going round and round in my head.

I mind the moment so well. That moment she found the fiddle. We'd been out in the fields all day, gathering the sheep, getting them ready for the shearing and Mum went into the byre to put something away, and the next thing I heard this scream and thought she'd fallen on something and rushed into the barn to find her jumping up and down there at the top of the stairs shouting, 'It was here after all! It was here after all!' And of course she told me all about it then and made sure I got proper lessons – I went to Miss Smart for violin and to that great local worthy, Duncan Bàn MacGillivray, for so-called traditional fiddle.

And Helen would always stand up at that point and begin diddling – 'Hai diddly hum di, hai diddly di... six-eight, up-and-down... fiddle ma ri!' What fantastic old tunes he had – wonderful old Gaelic tunes, many without name, as well as some very fine compositions of his own. It is no wonder that everything seemed lost when the fiddle was stolen.

She told me everything I've included and all the things that have been excluded because they didn't fit the story or the style. Sometimes she told them as conversation, sometimes as narrative, in real time and in recall, as of course did Alasdair and Katell and Big Roderick and all the rest. Their voices inhabit my empty house. Last night as I lay in the bath I remembered Margherita again and even tried to phone her, but there was no response. There is a peculiar loneliness in the unanswered call of a foreign ringtone.

This morning when I got up the mist was lying low over

the hills and moving over the loch and then a hare hopped across my garden. The hares were witches and Fearchar told of a man he knew who had shot one using an old sixpence as a bullet, but who then fled to Australia to escape her retribution. Nevertheless, he fell into a ravine once he arrived there. Some claimed he'd committed suicide, and I thought of the lone grave I'd stumbled across years ago up on the ridges of Meall Buidhe. I asked around and some folk said that it was the body of an English climber, but Bessie MacDonald, who knew about these things, told me that it was the body of 'a poor demented man who killed himself. A fellow MacRae, who belonged to Kintail but was down here working as a shepherd. He's buried up there out of sight of the sea.'

Suicides were interred out of sight of water for fear that the fish would abandon the rivers and lochs and ocean if they were within sight. Just as the remains of stillborn infants must be buried before sunrise or after sunset. There is a cure too for epilepsy, said old Bessie. 'You give the sufferer three drinks in the name of each person of the Trinity, from a running stream, with the skull of a suicide.'

All that is absent. By which I mean everything that is absent, which is not here, which is somewhere else. Elsewhere. The absence of the presence. The emptiness of the skull. The out-of-sightness of the suicide. The negative force which drives the fear. The drowned father. The lost violin. The boarded up boat. Helen. And this tracking-bone through which I write. Eilidh. Everything which makes life worthwhile, balanced, redeemable. The force that through the green fuse drives the flower drives my green age.

The mist rises off the loch. It ascends over the hills. The loch glitters, blue. The hills shine, silver. The boy and the girl on the bike were Helen and I. We cycled fast down the hill, freewheeling it toward the bottom and then jumped off without stopping, leaping on to the grass. We landed in a heap and the cycles themselves carried on, wobbling this way and that for a while, until they crashed off the road near the cattle grid where they lay for a while, four wheels spinning.

We laughed and held hands and raced across the green grass for a while until we reached the sand. There was a rock there and we stood on it, daring each other to jump. We finally agreed on a formula.

'I'll say ONE,' she said.

'And I'll say TWO,' I said. 'And then both of us will shout THREE!'

'ONE,' she said.

'TWO,' I replied.

'THREE,' we shouted, as we leapt together beyond the seaweed into the clear blue water.

15

OF COURSE IT gets lonely. But an old man is entitled to his dreams and hopes and memories, isn't he? Like King David, who of us would not like a firm-boned young concubine to cuddle up to in the night, to warm our ancient flesh? So we find her.

Sometimes I go out in the boat and let the wind ruffle the sail, just for the thrill of hearing the wind in the canvas and watching the way in which one moment I can tack this way, and then – with a slight twist of the tiller – that way. I read thrillers, and am a great admirer of Hammet who in the words of that other great writer, Raymond Chandler, 'gave murder back to the kind of people that commit it for reasons, not just to provide a corpse; and with the means at hand, not with hand-wrought duelling pistols, curare and tropical fish. He took murder out of the Venetian vase and dropped it into the alley.'

I wonder about the reasons too, not just about the corpse, and meditate about the means at hand, which is the giving of clues, signals and gestures. A young man asked a girl he knew, while she was leaning at an open window, if she would go out with him. She replied, 'I will, as soon as I have lifted the linen, lowered the glass, and covered the living with the dead.' The young boy despaired at the enormity of the conditions, gave up hope and sailed to foreign parts; and, returning at the end of three years, he heard she was now married to another, but was very unhappy. This grieved him, and on going to see her he asked her why she had rejected him. 'I didn't,' she replied. 'All I said was that I would go out with you, as soon as I lifted the linen cloth off the table, shut the window and smoored the fire. That did not take long, but by the time I'd done it, you were gone.'

I think constantly of those who lifted the linen, lowered the glass and covered the living with the dead. Old Alasdair and Katell themselves stranded out there in the glens of Aberdeenshire, and how every Thursday they would take the bus east through the small villages of the Mearns to finally arrive at Stonehaven when they could see the sea. They would lunch at the small Bay Café then walk down by the beach for the two hours they had before the bus returned inland. It's a fine sweep of a bay with a grand view of the North Sea and they would spend some time looking at the little yachts and skiffs and inshore fishing boats which still used the harbour. It had lovely clear promenades with wonderful breakwaters which gave good shelter to the little boats. After Easter the ice cream vendors would appear and Katell and Alasdair would then buy cones and walk arm in arm round the breakwater walls enjoying the scenes. When the spring and autumn gales came around they would stand in the shelter of the old boathouse watching the waves slapping against the harbour wall then thrashing, as the wind rose, across the barriers, spraying the cars and building with foam. Then in the summer all kinds of shows and sideshows arrived to brighten up the scene: clowns and little Punch and Judy shows and the annual fair with its music and dodgems. They would sometimes take the grandchildren up for the day with them and delight in their delights as the little ones went up-and-down and up-and-down on the dazzling horses on the carousel, and the bigger ones whooped and shouted as the were flung this-way-and-that on the wheels and helter-skelter. They always bought a fish supper at the end of the day and ate that sitting on the harbour wall just before the 6pm bus left to take them back in through the green straths.

And there are grandchildren, and perhaps even now their children, out there in America who know nothing of this. After a while the morning sun becomes a memory and places you knew, sometimes reluctantly, as a child become indistinct and hazy. You remember a wall somewhere and how the moss grew on the cornerstone but can't remember if there was a gate, and whether the stile that led up to the ash tree with the swing was painted green or blue. Other things replace memory and that grassy view towards the coral beach becomes overlaid with more recent images: do you remember how fast the cable cars in San Francisco moved when going downhill, and the taste of those fresh shrimps we ate that time in the Canaries? And you hear things, told by someone who was there, but it's like a far away sound, like vaguely watching a film while having a conversation with someone else.

Donald sometimes told of such things but they seemed to his children like a wooden story, a jigsaw for old people. I think often of the girl and the boy at the window, and how she said one thing and meant another, and how he heard one thing and understood another. The love we had was also spoken through the thin distance of a window to someone inches away.

I too will now set the table, open the window, and light the fire.

Some Other Books published by **LUATH PRESS**

Memory and Straw
Angus Peter Campbell
ISBN 978-1-92147-41-0 PBK £8.99

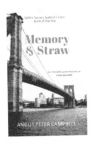

Gavin and Emma live in Manhattan. She's a musician. He works in Artificial Intelligence. He's good at his job – scarily good – researching human features to make more realistic mask-bots – non-human 'carers' for elderly people. When his enquiry turns personal he's forced to ask whether his own life is an artificial mask. He returns to England to look after his Grampa. Delves into his roots in the Highlands of Scotland. Reads old documents. Visits ruins. Borrows, plagiarises and invents. But when Emma tells him his proper work is to make a story out of glass and steel, not memory and straw, which path will he choose? This novel about the struggle for freedom and personal identity was Saltire Scottish Fiction Book of the Year, 2017.

A rich and humane novel.
ALLAN MASSIE, THE SCOTSMAN

This novel in English by Scotland's most renowned Gaelic novelist is possibly his best yet. SALTIRE SOCIETY

A remarkable book.
PHIL MILLER, THE HERALD

Archie and the North Wind
Angus Peter Campbell
ISBN 978-1906817-38-1 PBK £8.99

The old story has it that Archie, tired of the north wind, sought to extinguish it. Archie genuinely believes the old legends he was told as a child. Growing up on a small island off the Scottish coast and sheltered from the rest of the world, despite all the knowledge he gains as an adult, he still believes in the underlying truth of these stories.

To escape his mundane life, Archie leaves home to find the hole where the North Wind originates, to stop it blowing so harshly in winter. Funny, original and very moving, *Archie and the North Wind* demonstrates the raw power of storytelling.

Although every page is marked with some unquiet reflection, these are offset by amusing observations which give the novel a sparkle.
SCOTTISH REVIEW OF BOOKS

Details of these and other books published by Luath Press can be found at:
www.luath.co.uk

Luath Press Limited

committed to publishing well written books worth reading

LUATH PRESS takes its name from Robert Burns, whose little collie
Luath (*Gael.*, swift or nimble) tripped up Jean Armour at a wedding
and gave him the chance to speak to the woman who was to be his wife
and the abiding love of his life. Burns called one of the 'Twa Dogs'
Luath after Cuchullin's hunting dog in Ossian's *Fingal*.
Luath Press was established in 1981 in the heart of
Burns country, and is now based a few steps up
the road from Burns' first lodgings on
Edinburgh's Royal Mile. Luath offers you
distinctive writing with a hint of
unexpected pleasures.
Most bookshops in the UK, the US, Canada,
Australia, New Zealand and parts of Europe,
either carry our books in stock or can order them
for you. To order direct from us, please send a £sterling
cheque, postal order, international money order or your
credit card details (number, address of cardholder and
expiry date) to us at the address below. Please add post
and packing as follows: UK – £1.00 per delivery address;
overseas surface mail – £2.50 per delivery address; overseas airmail
– £3.50 for the first book to each delivery address, plus £1.00 for each
additional book by airmail to the same address. If your order is a gift,
we will happily enclose your card or message at no extra charge.

Luath Press Limited
543/2 Castlehill
The Royal Mile
Edinburgh EH1 2ND
Scotland
Telephone: +44 (0)131 225 4326 (24 hours)
email: sales@luath.co.uk
Website: www.luath.co.uk